A First for Ivy Pritchard

by

Maeve Kim

Love Stories of the Burlington Bird Club, Book One

A First for Ivy Pritchard

Contact Information: info@thewildrosepress.com

Cover Art by *The Wild Rose Press, Inc.*

The Wild Rose Press, Inc.
PO Box 708
Adams Basin, NY 14410-0708
Visit us at www.thewildrosepress.com

Publishing History
First Edition, 2024
Trade Paperback ISBN 978-1-5092-5615-0
Digital ISBN 978-1-5092-5616-7

Love Stories of the Burlington Bird Club, Book One
Published in the United States of America

Dedication

TO THE BIRDS
To the robins that delighted my two little daughters and me;
To the little nuthatch that comforted me when I was afraid for our lives;
To the distant birds that gave me courage to travel and stay in remote cabins and walk hundreds of miles alone in nature;
To the local birds that convinced me to offer classes and nature walks;
To the ducks, herons and gnatcatchers that brought an extraordinary man to one of my walks;
To the birds we now watch together, hand in hand.

An earlier version of this book was self-published several years ago, but the characters of Ivy and Hugh didn't leave my thoughts. They haunted me, waking me up in the night with single sentences and whole chapters that were so much better than the original. I began to feel they were real people, not my inventions, and that they wanted me to retell their love story and this time do it right! I am tremendously grateful to Wild Rose Press for giving me (and them) a chance.

Praise for *A First for Ivy Pritchard*

"This beautifully woven story invites you to glimpse the extraordinary in the ordinary, following the stumbles of our heroine in life and love (and birding)."
~ *Elizabeth Spinney, writer and board member of Birds of Vermont Museum*

"It isn't often that a novel grabs me on page one and makes me invested in the characters from the beginning. This book did! It has a strong focus on the natural world and believable, lovable characters. And it has a story that sucks the reader in and compels them to keep turning the pages."
~ *Steven Shepard, author of 98 non-fiction books, four novels, and many articles. He hosts the popular Podcast, The Natural Curiosity Project.*

"An enjoyable, memorable read with beautiful descriptions of the natural world. Avid birders and non-birders alike will delight in this sweet story."
~ *Julie Cadwallader Staub, Author of Wing Over Wing*

Chapter One

The summer of the lost warbler was Ivy's thirty-fourth year of being alone. As her high school classmates started dating. All through college. And all through her twenties. Alone.

It was even worse when she turned thirty. She had felt humiliated, as if anyone with half a brain should have figured out by age thirty how *not* to be alone.

But somehow, just about the time of her thirty-second birthday, like a wonderful birthday present from an unknown friend, Ivy got tired of fretting about being alone. Tired of being embarrassed. She stopped aching, stopped imagining and dreaming and hoping. Stopped looking at every new man to see if he might be The One.

And almost immediately, as if she was giving off some calming hormonal scent, people stopped bugging her. Her aunt's monthly e-mails no longer included news about the bachelor neighbor. Her best customer stopped telling her when his brother from Seattle was going to be in town. The whole world seemed to have stopped wondering if Ivy Pritchard was ever going to meet a man and settle down.

By the spring leading to the summer of the warbler, Ivy had magically evolved from pitiful and desperate, to independent and eccentric. And being an independent and eccentric loner was absolutely perfect for a woman in her thirties who was a birdwatcher and who ran a store for other birdwatchers.

****

The last customers weren't in any hurry to leave Ivy's Optics and Accessories for the Dedicated Birder. Ivy wasn't in any hurry to chase them out either, even though the manager of the bookstore at the end of the mall had turned off his lights and was pulling the iron grate across the front of his shop.

"I'll be careful with them, Ivy, but what if they accidentally get wet? What about fog?"

She grinned at the skinny, intense boy in front of her. "Sean, this pair of binoculars will be fine in whatever Vermont throws at them. Fog, mist, rain, sleet, or snow. Just don't drop them into a lake."

"I would *never* do that."

She looked up at the boy's grandfather. "Charlie, this is a truly awesome birthday present."

Charlie's big hand ruffled the boy's hair. "Deserves it. Been birdin' since he was five."

"Four and a half."

"Four and a half then."

"And I already got almost a hundred birds on my life list. Species, I mean."

"That's impressive, Sean. Very."

"Uses my old binocs. Big, heavy." He nodded toward the pair in the boy's hands. "Nowhere near as good as those. You set, Sean? These're what you want?"

"Yes!"

Standing between the two of them, Ivy looked like a tropical flower in bright green pants, satiny blue shirt, and silk vest in stained glass colors. The overhead light shone on her close-cut cap of dark curls, the boy's wheat-colored mop, and the man's once-yellow hair, now a blend of silver and gold.

"Molly, would you ring up this totally awesome gift for our friends?"

The fourth person in the store was a tiny woman whose impish face was almost hidden in a bouncy mass of white curls.

"Sean, these are wonderful. You are one lucky dude."

His grin stretched all over his face. "Don't I know it! I'm gonna bring these on the FATSO walk!"

"Of course you are! And you'll be able to see every single feather on every single bird!"

F. A. T. S. O. The first letters of First And Third Sunday Outings, the regular bird walks of the Montpelier Branch of the venerable Burlington Bird Club. For three years now, Ivy had led one of the club's two monthly outings, and Molly and Charlie were two of her most loyal regulars.

Molly sighed. "Ahhh. Young birders always make me misty. So young, so full of energy and excitement and hope."

"Like you don't have those same qualities."

Molly grinned. "I do, don't I? I constantly astonish myself. My face keeps getting older and older while my inside feelings are going in the opposite direction." She opened the cash register and started counting twenties. "Retiring was the best thing I ever did."

"Glad to hear that my quiet store is better than a big city trauma center."

Molly set the cash on the counter and held out her left hand, palm up. "Birds, nature, birders." She held out her right hand. "Gun shots and sucking chest wounds." She looked from one hand to the other. "No contest." She put the twenties into a bank deposit bag, made a note on a scrap of paper, and started counting tens. "So, what's on for the FATSO birders this weekend, Ivy? I hope it'll be better than the disastrous Moose Bog trip two weeks ago."

"How could Moose Bog be disastrous? That's a great place!"

The little woman leaned her elbows on the counter. With her mischievous face and her chinos and hiking shoes, she looked like a child wearing a curly white wig.

"Where do I start?" She sighed. "You heard that the always egregious Josef was a substitute driver for the always delightful Jack, right?" Molly exaggerated the YUH sound at the start of the name, her face twisted with distaste. "Well, Yosef got lost and we ended up almost at Canadian Customs, then he got the van stuck, and then we saw not a single bird. Not one."

Molly suddenly let out her characteristic laugh, a loud raucous whinny that didn't seem to fit her tiny self. "Josef even wore a special hat for the trip to the frozen northlands. A huge fur thing, like something in a Russian movie."

Ivy's soft chortle was a contrast to her friend's loud mirth. "*Doctor Zhivago*."

"Exactly." Molly sighed and shook her head. "It's sad that such a handsome man is such an unmitigated jerk."

"Well, it sounds like the jerk set a very low standard for me, for the next trip. I'm thinking of a late winter eagle hunt along Lake Champlain."

"Good choice." Molly zipped the fabric bag closed. "Want me to do the deposit tonight? I'm heading downtown anyway, and it's out of your way."

"That would be great, Moll. Thanks."

****

Downtown wasn't out of Ivy's way. Not at all. She could have walked from where she lived to the bank and back home in twenty minutes. But no one, not even her only employee and best friend, knew that. Like everyone else, Molly thought Ivy was still living in her parents' old apartment above the East Montpelier library. Not one of them knew that she was living, secretly and illicitly, in the storage area behind her shop at the Capitol City Mall.

Ivy had never planned on living at the mall. It was just one night, the night after her father's funeral. She planned on going back to the apartment to continue sorting and packing but she found herself at her shop and she spent the night in the back room on the musty-smelling couch that a previous shopkeeper had brought for his dog to nap on. The next day, she dragged the old couch out the back door into the parking lot, left it near the dumpsters, and bought a daybed.

The daybed made the back room comfortable. The toilet made it possible. Ivy's Optics and Accessories for the Dedicated Birder was the only store in the mall with its own lavatory. The very first person to lease the space, way back in the sixties, had paid for the john with his own money because he said he couldn't do his business with anyone listening.

Three days after the funeral, Ivy stood in the back room and thought about spending her free hours looking for an apartment.

"This is as big as a lot of motel rooms," she muttered. "I can just reheat stuff in the microwave, stuff from the co-op or Jorge's or Guido's. It'll be just a few

5

days."

A few days stretched into a few weeks. And then months. Now she'd been there almost two years, and it didn't even feel odd any more to rely on the twenty-four-hour gym for showers. To make up the daybed early every morning and check that the bedspread hid the two big plastic boxes of clothes stored underneath. To lock the metal cabinet that held her books and shampoo and laundry detergent and winter boots and dirty clothes, so Molly wouldn't accidentally open it. It all felt normal—until Ivy thought about anyone else knowing. Then it felt just plain weird.

****

The Burlington Bird Club had over thirty members, with six or eight regulars for FATSO walks. No one new had joined for years, so there was considerable curiosity when the group gathered for Ivy's March walk and Molly brought with her an unfamiliar man.

"Everyone, this is a neighbor of mine. Hugh MacDougal. He's interested in birding. Hugh, you'll get to know everyone in time. For now, this is Ivy, our trip leader."

The man was tall, raw-boned, and rigid. He stood with his chin tipped slightly up, the skin stretched taut over his cheekbones. In the direct sun, his close-cropped beard and mustache glinted red, several shades lighter than his thick hair.

"Great name!" Ivy grinned at him. "With that reddish hair and your size and build, you'd look right at home on some moor somewhere, wearing a kilt. And carrying a battle axe."

Not a muscle in his face moved.

Ivy tried again. "Are you a beginning birder?"

"I watch my feeders." His voice was deep and slightly hoarse.

"Would you like some pointers about using your binoculars?" He looked so forbidding that she found herself talking faster. "To—um—so you can get the most out of them?"

"I know how to use binoculars."

His eyes were as cold and distant as his voice.

"Okay. Good. So." Ivy turned to Molly. "Do you know if anyone else is coming?"

"Nope. All here." Her eyes flicked toward the new man. "All happy."

Ivy turned so she could see the whole group. "There are lots of diving ducks on the lake right now, and at least one eagle has been seen regularly right here at Button Bay. We'll hang out for a while and then maybe try a few more spots."

Brilliant sun sparkled off the fresh snow, off the ice rimming the bay, and off the choppy open water farther out. The pines on two small islands looked impossibly blue-green, the sky looked impossibly blue, and the fast-moving clouds looked impossibly white.

As Ivy wiggled into her wind pants, she heard Molly let out a subdued whoop.

"We could not have timed this better if we'd tried!"

Two Bald Eagles stood on the snow-covered ice not far from shore. An adult bird, white head and tail glowing in the bright sun, was crouched over an unmoving pile of feathers. Bright drops of blood gleamed on the ice. Behind the adult, a dark brown immature bird was taking nervous sideways steps, repeatedly stretching its neck toward the carcass but always withdrawing.

"The immature really wants some of that duck. Mallard? Yeah." Josef spoke in a guttural whisper although it was clear that the big birds on the ice weren't interested in or alarmed by the watching humans. "This is gonna be one great photo. A money shot." He pulled a digital camera from a pocket along with a small black device. "My new toy. Adaptor. Don't have to bring my big camera. Gettin' in on that thare digiscoping thang." He screwed the camera and adaptor to the end of a spotting scope and bent to plan his photo.

Beck watched him for a silent moment and then let out a little explosive puff of air. "There goes my chance to use *my* birthday present." She turned toward the lake. "May I take a look through your scope, Ivy?"

"Be my guest."

As Ivy made room for her friend, she noticed that the new guy was standing silent, still a little apart from the group, watching Josef with his eyes somber and puzzled.

****

After many minutes, the adult eagle straightened, shook itself all over, flapped its impressive wings, and took off toward the open water. The younger bird immediately moved over what was left of the mallard and began tearing it apart with its hooked bill.

"The adult might be full, finally. Or maybe he's just had all his favorite parts and now is going to get himself another duck."

"Sitting duck."

"True."

Just beyond the edge of the ice was a huge raft of ducks in various patterns of dark and white. The birds were in constant motion, rising and falling on the waves, diving and popping up again, chasing each other along the top of the water.

"There must be two or three thousand out there."

"All-you-can-eat buffet for an eagle."

"What's out there, Ivy?"

"You tell us, Sean. Your granddad says you've been studying up. So—What's out there?"

The youngster glanced sideways at her and squared his shoulders. "Okay. So. There's Scaup. They're the ones that are black fore and aft." He grinned. "That's what Grampa says."

"Excellent."

"And goldeneye. Common Goldeneye. They've got white sides too but they're smaller. And the males have that white dot on their cheek. Ummm. Oh! And there's a few Buffleheads with that big white thingee on their face."

Jack clapped the boy on the shoulder, his wind-reddened face cheerful and excited. "Way to go, Sean. Ivy, let me at your scope just for a minute… Ah! I thought so. Love is in the air. Courtship behavior! Get a load of the goldeneye drakes."

Several of the little males were energetically throwing their heads back and pointing their bills at the sky.

Molly whinnied. "I always wonder how they don't get whiplash doing that!"

"They can't, Molly. It is a law of nature." Jack looked around at the group and raised one finger, pretend-solemn. "That which we guys do for love might embarrass us, might humiliate us, might even make us look like fools and morons, but it will never cause permanent damage." He laughed. "When I was courting

Rose, I wanted to take her on some manly outdoor activity. I thought birding wasn't manly so I decided we should try geocaching. I would wow her with my adept use of map, compass, and GPS." He twisted his mouth comically. "I got us lost and ended up stepping off a cliff into thin air."

"Oh, no! Did Rose fall too?"

"No. No. Rose stayed at the top and watched as her manly suitor rolled and bounced downhill and landed on his butt in a stream. Lost my GPS, and a lot of my dignity. But I did not break a single one of my own bones. Which proves what I was saying: We guys are protected from injury when we're doing something for love."

Molly gave a soft whinnying laugh. "Rose might not have fallen off the cliff, Jack, but she fell for you, even without manly backwoods skills."

"She did. She did." Jack shook his head slowly from side to side. "And I have never stopped marveling about that."

Ivy was still watching the ducks through her binoculars. "The Goldeneyes have been courting for several months now. Takes lots of time and energy."

Beck snorted. "Energy. Time and energy both." She looked flustered when everyone but Josef turned toward her, but her words were as precise and measured as always. "And for many of them it's all wasted. That is a good life lesson: It takes a birdbrain to get that excited about finding a mate for just a few months."

Ivy glanced toward Josef but he seemed oblivious, still bent over his camera, muttering to himself.

"I wonder if there's anything unusual in the raft. Barrow's Goldeneye, maybe? Long-tailed Duck?"

"Yeah!" Jack, as always, responded with enthusiasm. "Or a Tufted Duck!"

A half hour passed before Ivy felt a tap on her shoulder. She turned to find the new guy, his back to the others, staring intently at a small group of trees.

"There's something in the middle. Two feet straight down from twelve o'clock."

Through her binoculars, Ivy could see two messy shapes side by side on a horizontal branch.

"Oh, good eye. Really good eye. They must have a nest in that tree."

"What?"

"Barred Owls." She turned the scope, focused, then stepped back and raised her binoculars again. "Look through the scope. You can just see the nest above them, where that big branch heads off to the right." She turned her head and raised her voice a little. "Barred Owls. Two of them."

Ducks and eagles temporarily forgotten, the birders turned and Charlie focused his scope on the owls.

"They look like rag mops," Molly said. "With big eyes."

"Yes!" Josef pushed by Ivy, jostling her with his elbow. "This is what I came for. Way better than distant dots of ducks!" He fiddled with his scope and camera and went on talking, more to himself than to anyone else. "Oh, yes. The money shot. Good light. Both in one frame. Yes indeed." He walked several yards across the frozen field, holding the tripod in front of him, stopping often to refocus and snap more pictures. The owls swiveled their heads, watching the man's approach.

"Not too close, Josef," Ivy called. "With the nest right there, they can be easily agitated."

"Nah. They don't care." He kept walking, closer and closer to the two owls.

Charlie made a noise that sounded like a snarl and took off after the photographer, who was now within twenty yards of the owls. The group on the bluff couldn't hear what he said but they saw Josef whirl around, his face tight and angry. He shouldered the tripod so quickly that the metal legs hit the other man in the chest and then he stalked across the field. Seconds later they all heard the car engine.

"Well." Beck's voice was calm and flat. "It looks very much like I have been abandoned."

"He'll be back, Beck."

"That is highly unlikely."

Charlie's face was grim as he returned.

"What did you tell him?"

"Same as you would've, Ivy. BBC-sponsored trip. No harassing birds."

"He's not going home, you know."

"Beg pardon?"

"Josef will stop a little way south of here and give us all time to leave. Then he will come back. And he will just about climb up into that tree to get a good picture." Beck's little laugh sounded more like a gasp. "Gotta get the money shot… I'll need a ride home. I'm done. May I go sit in your car?"

"Of course, but…" Ivy looked at Beck's face. "Of course. Here are the keys."

The group watched in silence as Beck stumbled across the frozen hummocks toward the parking lot. And then Hugh MacDougal spoke for the first time since he'd found the owls, his deep voice almost growling. "Is Rebecca in danger in her home?"

"Pardon? Oh. Beck. I don't think Rebecca's really her name. She spells it B.E.C.K." Ivy looked back toward the cars. "Josef is horrible but none of us think he's a physical threat."

The new man made a noise deep in his throat and turned away.

"Can't we vote him out or something?" Sean's young voice broke twice in that short question.

Jack gave a small laugh. "Great idea. Every one of us would be happier."

"How come she brings *him*?"

"Well, they live together. And Josef says he's interested. She couldn't really leave him out."

"Course she could! Just say 'Stay, Josef'. Like talking to a dog."

"Ah, Sean." Molly shook her head, her blue eyes dark and troubled. "It doesn't make sense why people stay in bad situations, but they do. Often."

The boy frowned. "Maybe she needs his money, like rent or something."

"Other way around." Charlie snorted. "Far as I can tell Josef teaches a few art classes, when he can. Tries to sell his photos. Beck's a hydrologist for the state. Good job."

Sean was still looking toward the parking lot. "The first time I met her, I thought she looked like Sacajawea."

"I can see that. Tall. Weathered. And all that dark hair." Ivy zipped her scope case closed. "Josef must have some redeeming qualities. In addition to his looks, I mean. Beck must see something good."

Charlie snorted. "Nope. I'm bettin' it's nothing but looks."

Molly sighed. "He is well-built and handsome. And

13

a bit dangerous-looking. Lots of women would be awed if he started paying attention to them. And then they'd wake up one morning and find themselves saddled with a self-centered ass who's happy to sponge off them for house, food, clothes—basically everything."

Charlie frowned fiercely as he looked across the bluff at the woman just visible in the passenger seat of Ivy's car. "Women in their thirties get desperate."

Chapter Two

While the FATSO group was standing on a windy bluff, watching diving ducks, the tiny bird that would change Ivy's life was flitting about in a forest canopy almost 3000 miles away. Its lemon-yellow breast made an ever-moving splash of color against dark pines.

Children yelled triumphantly from the tops of fantastic tumbles of rock. Teenagers dared each other to jump into pools formed by cascades as high as seven-story buildings. Adults walked, talked, laughed, flirted, spread out picnic lunches. Not one of the human visitors to Parque Natural Mexiquillo noticed the little bird.

At about the same time as the birding group got back to their homes with their minds on hot showers and hot suppers, the bird stopped feeding and started flying. It flew all night, sometimes in darkness and sometimes with white wing bars flashing in pale moonlight.

The sky around it was full of northbound migrants: thrushes, warblers, flycatchers. Many would stop in the mountains and canyons of Arizona, New Mexico, and west Texas, would choose and announce their territories, would find mates and raise young. Others were just beginning journeys that would take them all the way to the Canadian tundra. The gray and lemon-yellow bird from the Parque Natural Mexiquillo was heading for the Arizona canyon where, the previous spring, it had hatched, fledged, and tried its wings for the first time.

Chapter Three

"I'm looking for a binocular strap."

Ivy was sitting cross-legged on the floor in the children's section of her shop, unpacking wooden jigsaw puzzles of Vermont birds. She looked up and scrambled to her feet.

Whatever-his-name-was, the new man from last week's walk, was standing at the end of the aisle, bigger and craggier indoors than he had looked in the field.

"Oh. I didn't know this was your store."

Ivy pointed at the sign over the door. *Ivy's Optics and Accessories for the Dedicated Birder.*

"Oh. Yes." He looked around. "I need a binocular strap."

"Straps and binocular harnesses are right over here." She led him to a shelf in the back corner of the shop. "Most birders prefer harnesses."

"I came in for a strap."

"A harness will take the stress off the back of your neck so you can bird for many hours without even noticing the binocular weight." She tilted her head and smiled at him. "So if you happen to become addicted to your new hobby, you can do so painlessly."

He looked at her without any expression on his face. "I came in for a strap."

"Okay then." She pointed to three boxes. "I'd recommend one with good padding."

"I'll take that into consideration."

Ivy walked away, frowning. She stood behind the counter and watched as the man read the boxes of every strap on the shelf. He finally selected one, walked across the shop, put the box on the counter, got out his wallet, paid and left without saying another word.

"Fun person," she muttered.

****

"Oh goody, Molly. Your surly Scot is here again."

The new man was standing in the small parking lot at Brookside Nature Park, his binoculars hanging from his brand-new padded neck strap.

Molly waved gaily as she clambered out of Ivy's little Fiat, and the new guy responded with a curt nod. A few yards away, Charlie was getting his scope and tripod out of a beat-up SUV. His grandson Sean catapulted from the passenger seat and immediately raised his binoculars to his eyes, rapidly moving his head as if he wanted to see every branch on every tree in the next ten seconds.

"Jack said he might be a few minutes late. I don't know about Josef and Beck."

"They're not coming. They're—"

"Whoa!" Sean suddenly whistled. "Wicked wheels."

A little Smart Car was coming down the hill, the front decorated with two perfectly round eyes surrounded by brownish-green scales.

Ivy's delighted peal of laughter and Molly's whinny greeted Jack as he all but threw himself out of the tiny car and turned with a flourish, his hands spread to show off the car's new paint job.

"Jack! I love it! It's a chubby sturgeon!"

17

"Yup. I've been fighting with zoning for a full year now about a sign, and now I don't need one." He turned, laughing. "My car is my sign."

"I don't get it."

Charlie tousled his grandson's hair. "Mr. Carmichael makes ale and beer, Sean. Brand name Chubby Sturgeon. You know. Sturgeon. Fish."

Molly walked a few steps and looked at the lettering on the side of the car. "Great advertising, Jack. Eye-catching, tasteful, *and* artistic."

"I think so." The round little man turned to the group, bouncing a little on his toes with pleasure. "I truly do think so!"

****

When they got to the beaver pond, Ivy and Charlie set up their tripods and uncovered the spotting scopes.

"We'll stop here for a while," Ivy said quietly. "There's a Canada Goose in this scope, guarding his mate. There might be turtles sunning on a log or some ducks or perhaps a heron." She focused her scope and stepped back. "When you're not using one of the scopes, there's plenty of activity in the woods behind us. Chickadees, nuthatches, woodpeckers, maybe even some early warblers. And Ruby-crowned Kinglets. They show up here every year during spring migration. There's a small flock of them near us right now."

Sean was suddenly at her elbow, his fiercely scowling eyebrows just visible over the top of his binoculars.

"Don't use your binocs at first, Sean. Just scan the trees. Look for movement. Once you've located a bird, then you can raise your binocs."

"They're tiny, right?"

"Really tiny. Smaller than a chickadee. Drab olive color with pale eye rings. Just look for movement. There! In the two trees to the left of you. Now they moved right. Kinglets never stop moving. Never. Not even for a second." Ivy glanced around her. "Molly's on one. Watch where she's focusing."

"Two over here too." Jack was using the low raspy whisper that he reserved for Ivy's walks. "Yes! The flash!"

"Flash?"

Ivy whispered, "The crown. It's a little tuft of feathers that the birds erect when they're excited or angry. It's actually red-orange, not ruby-colored."

"Tiny neon sign flashing. Like in a diner window." Jack opened and closed his hand several times to show something flashing on and off. "Eat Here. Eat Here. Eat Here."

Sean raised his binoculars and made a noise in his throat. "Got one! On that dead branch."

"Hugh, have you found one yet?"

"No."

"There's one at two o'clock in that white birch. Now it's at four o'clock. It just flew down and to the left."

He grunted.

"There's another almost over your head."

He tipped his head up and Ivy saw his eyes follow the tiny bird as it flew.

"Did you see it?"

"Briefly."

"Have faith. You'll get a good look eventually. If not today, then some other time."

He glanced at her from the corner of his eye, unsmiling.

****

With the parking lot visible in the distance, the group was strung out along the path, Jack and Sean ahead of the others and the new man lagging behind.

Molly whinnied. "Jack's having the time of his life. He's got another kid to bird with!"

"Jack is definitely a kid at heart." Ivy turned to the silent man beside her. "Have you been on one of Jack's FATSO trips yet, Hugh?"

He shook his head.

"They go in cars. And while they're driving from bird to bird, those cars just about explode with babble." Ivy watched as Jack said something that dissolved Sean in laughter. "I really appreciate how he keeps it in for my walks."

The two in front stopped walking and raised their binoculars in unison, then Sean looked back and made an urgent gesture. "Grampa!"

A big bird was coming toward them from the direction of the beaver pond, gliding silently on broad wings, only a few feet above the treetops. As it got closer, the birders could see the apricot-colored belly.

Molly breathed, "The Red-shouldered Hawk. This trip is officially complete."

When the hawk was almost directly overhead, it made a lazy circle above them, its barred tail and the rich russet on its wings clearly visible against the sky. Then it screamed, a repeated downward keeee-ur. They all watched, frozen in place, as the hawk flew out of sight behind the trees.

Jack turned to the group, his round face glowing with excitement. "Our own BBC bird! I am inspired to give a little oration, so that the youngster who is birding with us today can know exactly how special that bird is." He cleared his throat and squared his shoulders. "Red-shouldered Hawks do not over-winter in Vermont. They just do not. That's what all the guidebooks say. All the range maps. All the experts even. But there's been a pair here in this park every winter, all winter, for five years now. They were first seen and first documented in the winter by BBC members. Their nest was first discovered and photographed by BBC members. They are our very own hawks. Seeing one calls for a spirited round of celebratory fist bumps!"

Molly laughed. "Only you would think of fist bumps, Jack!"

The group spread out again, Jack and Sean again in front. Ivy almost forgot the new man and was startled to hear his deep voice behind her.

"You asked why I come on these walks."

"Yes?"

"I like birds. I see more when there's a knowledgeable group."

"Oh." She stopped and let him catch up with her. "That's a very good reason."

"I appreciate your being patient about the kinglet."

"You're welcome."

His brown eyes studied her face for a moment, then he nodded.

****

Ivy put the scope and tripod in the back seat of her car and turned toward Molly.

"So, what's the story with Mr. Sunshine?"

"Hugh?" Molly looked across the parking lot at the spare figure shedding his hat and binoculars. "I really don't know him well. He already lived in the neighborhood when Ed and I moved in but he hasn't shown up at any of the community barbecues."

"Why does that not surprise me?"

"At first I figured him for retired military, although he'd be pretty young for retirement. He always holds himself as if he's getting ready to salute or be saluted or something. And his mustache and beard always look like they've just been clipped."

"His hair's too long."

"Well, yes. But maybe even an army barber would be reluctant to cut all that richness. It'd be sinful, like giving a buzz cut to a mink."

The two women watched as Hugh lifted his shoulders and rolled them a little, as if they hurt.

"I don't think they allow beards in the military, Molly."

"Well then, he looks like he belongs in Ulysses S. Grant's military. He'd be in command, though, not an everyday grunt."

"Definitely. I can't see him taking orders."

Molly slid into the passenger seat. "I think he jogs down to Hubbard Park and back just about every morning, no matter what the weather. Even his running looks military. No ear buds, no iPod, no music. Just grim face and pumping legs. He usually doesn't carry anything but one day last month he was wearing a fanny pack. It was partly unzipped and I saw binoculars. So I stopped him and told him his pack was open, and I also told him about the BBC."

"And he bubbled over with excitement."

Molly looked at her wryly. "Yeah." She watched Hugh get into his car. "But I thought he showed a spark of interest. And he's here, again. Although I wouldn't say he's having the time of his life."

"But he found the owls last time. And he just thanked me for showing him the kinglet."

Molly turned to her, surprised. "He thanked you?"

Ivy nodded. "He did. And he looked like a real birder today."

****

Ivy credited a binocular harness for her ownership of the store.

Two days after her mother's second stroke, and one day after Ivy said goodbye to her beloved tree house, she wandered through the Capitol City Mall and noticed a Part-Time Help Wanted sign in the window of an optics store. Inside, two men were deep in discussion next to a case full of cameras and lenses. The only other person in the store was a woman who was staring at a harness hanging from a wooden peg. She took the harness down and pulled it over her arms and head and then made a frustrated noise when one of the elastic straps ended up across her throat.

"May I help? I have the same model at home."

"Oh! I thought it was obvious but now I seem to be all tangled up."

"Raise your arms."

"Ahh. Thank you. Can you show me how it's supposed to work?"

"Easy as pie, although not obvious at first glance." Ivy quickly put the harness on herself and then took it off again and handed it over.

"Okay. Let's try… Ahh. This feels really comfy." She gave Ivy a wide smile. "My sister and I are going on a walking tour in Ireland in a few weeks. For twenty-one days."

"That sounds wonderful."

"She's the birder in the family. Her birthday is tomorrow so I decided to get her a harness so she can carry her binoculars all day without ending up with a big red line on the back of her neck."

"Excellent idea. No birder I know would ever go back to a strap after trying one of these."

"You'd recommend this brand?"

"They're all pretty much alike, I think, but that's the one I have."

"Okay then." The woman reached out and picked up a box, and then a second box. "Might as well get one for me too. Peg says she's bringing her back-up binoculars for me to use."

After the baby-faced clerk finalized the woman's harness purchase, he turned to Ivy.

"Nice salesmanship."

Ivy smiled at the scrubbed, boyish face.

"No salesmanship. Just the truth."

"Thank you anyway. If you hadn't been here to interact with that woman, she might have left in frustration. Instead she bought two items and is likely to come back." He held out his hand. "I'm the shop's owner. Bill."

Ten minutes later, Ivy accepted a part-time job at northern Vermont's only birding store. And two years later, she bought it.

Chapter Four

The high bare peak looming above the trees was already touched by red-gold dawn, but sun wouldn't brighten the canyon floor for several hours. A tiny Elf Owl called to its mate as it glided back to the nest after the last hunting foray of the night.

The yellow-and-gray Grace's Warbler arrived, hungry, and spent several hours gleaning insects. Then the bird chose a perch high in an ancient cottonwood and began announcing that it was in possession of a desirable territory and was seeking a mate. The ascending trill from the top of the cottonwood tree was a challenge that could not be ignored. An older, more experienced bird had already claimed that tree, and it flew at the new arrival with feet extended and wings beating wildly. For most of the morning, the young warbler tried singing and the other bird attacked it.

By the time the noon sun shone into the deep canyon from directly overhead, the young warbler gave up. It flew down the canyon and kept going, looking for another place where it could find a mate and raise young warblers.

The young warbler followed the streambed to an area with fewer piñons and more cactus. Below, people called out to each other, yelled, ran, played games, lit charcoal fires, and cooked food, filled the air with smoke and noise. It was too much like Parque Natural

Mexiquillo. It was not a place to nest and raise young.

The bird left the canyon and again flew northeast. When dawn came, there was nothing below but flat land, cactus, mesquite, and oil pumpers. No shaded canyons, no pine trees, no streams. The bird found a small, wooded park surrounded by houses where it rested and fed for several hours, and then it flew on.

Chapter Five

"Ahhhhh. What a great walk. I absolutely love this place."

The first FATSO trip in May, an annual pilgrimage to a wildlife refuge tucked in the northwest corner of the state, always attracted additional BBC members. Fourteen birders were spread out along the old railroad embankment, heading back to the cars.

"Me too." Ivy grinned at Molly. "So, what was your BOD?"

"My Bird of the Day?" Molly's white curls were almost blinding as they walked from shade into bright sunshine. "I guess I'd have to choose a group, not just one single bird. Northern Water-thrushes. I've never seen or heard so many in one place in my entire life."

"Whoa there, you two. It's too early to be talking BODs. The day's not even over yet!" With the parking lot in sight, Jack was back to his regular speaking style: loud, strong, fast, and excited. "We've got a good tenth of a mile to go before the cars! Who knows what might show up? Any minute now, we might see a Northern Harrier. No! We might see a harrier chasing a Merlin that's chasing a Grasshopper Sparrow. We'd get three in one!"

"Do you think that's possible? Three in one?"

"Sean, that's what makes birding fun. The possibilities!"

"Grampa, what's your Bird of the Day?" Sean shot a quick glance at Jack. "So far?"

"Me? Ospreys. Settin' up housekeeping. When I was a kid, an older birder told me I better take a good look at an Osprey. 'Cause they'd all be gone in a couple years."

"Why? Hunting?"

"DDT. You know about DDT, right?"

Sean nodded.

"Well, Ospreys were just about wiped out. Along with Bald Eagles and Peregrine Falcons and Common Loons."

Molly nodded. "And now all four are real success stories here in Vermont."

"Always hear about humans screwing things up. Destroying nature. But this time humans tried to undo the harm they'd done. Satisfying."

"I love the passion in Charlie's voice." Ivy spoke quietly. "It's good for Sean to hear."

"He's good for Sean. Period."

"True."

"There's no dad in the picture, right?"

"Right."

They slowed down so Ivy could maneuver her tripod under a large tree that was leaning across the trail. "This was a successful outing in another way too, Molly. Your grouchy neighbor not only offered to drive; he actually volunteered two whole sentences."

"Wait. Let me guess what they were. Get away from me. I'll bite."

"Yikes. You weren't so negative about him before."

"I know." Molly sighed. "And it's not really me to be negative, not about anybody. But the same thing happens every single morning. I'm outdoors watering the flowers or getting the newspaper and he runs by and I wave and smile. And he nods. Curtly." She made her eyes huge and dramatic. "I'm a delightful person! People adore me! No one just nods curtly when I'm trying to be friendly!" She lifted her chin in the direction of the small parking lot where Hugh and several others were already waiting. "But *he* does. It pisses me off. Royally!"

Hugh had put his binoculars on top of his car and was unbuttoning his long-sleeved shirt and yanking it free of his pants.

"However, Ivy, that is one nice bod."

"I haven't really noticed."

"Well, notice now."

He shrugged off his shirt, revealing an off-white pullover that looked to Ivy like the top half of a set of long johns.

"If he weren't so damn unapproachable, I would strongly recommend that you do just that."

Ivy was looking at the man's long legs, wondering if he was wearing the bottom half of the long johns.

"Do just what, Molly?"

"Approach. With intent."

Ivy was rescued from answering by a sudden shout from Jack.

"Get a move on! We're all hot. We're all thirsty. We're only minutes from Bobby's Pub." He tilted his head back and bellowed, "And we all know what's at Bobby's Pub!"

At least a dozen voices answered immediately. "Jack's brewskis!"

****

Hugh waited until Molly and Ivy were in his car

before asking, "Jack's brewskis?"

Ivy leaned forward from the back seat. "Jack has been brewing ales and beers for years now."

"Oh. Yes. The car."

"Exactly. Chubby Sturgeon. His cousin Bobby runs a restaurant in Swanton and, of course, he serves Jack's brews." She leaned back and fastened her seat belt. "And he loves us birders."

Hugh pulled out of the lot and fell in line behind the other cars. "Are Jack's brews any good?"

"Very."

He glanced up at the rearview mirror and met Ivy's eyes. "What's best?"

"Do you prefer dark or light?"

"Dark. But not as dark as stout."

"Ah! A fellow traveler! Everybody but me likes the pale ales. For the likes of us, Hugh, Chubby Sturgeon Brown Ale is nectar of the gods."

****

Jack's cousin ushered the birders through the main dining room and through a wide doorway. "The traditional private room, at your service." He pulled out a chair at one end of the long table and turned to Ivy with a little bow. "And your traditional place, Miss Ivy, at the head of the table."

Molly sat down on Ivy's right. Somewhat to her surprise, Hugh took the seat on her left.

"Okay, birders." Jack stopped in the middle of lowering himself into the chair beside Hugh. "I phoned in an order for appetizers so we can start chowing down in a few seconds. What about you, Hugh? You a nacho man or a skins man?"

"Are those the only options?"

At that moment, a waitress plopped a pile of menus in the middle of the table.

"Hell, no. There's a full menu. But we always start with humongous plates of nachos and cheese. And fried potato skins with bacon and more cheese and about a quart of sour cream."

Molly laughed her distinctive descending whinny. "From the heart-healthy section of the menu."

Several people opened menus as Bobby and the waitress started taking drink orders.

"I want the brown ale." Ivy turned to the tall man sitting next to her. "Hugh, if you're not sure, you can wait and try mine before you order."

He looked up at the waitress. "Give me the same." He opened a menu and lowered his voice. "Other than nachos and potato skins, what's good?"

"It's all good. Soups are made right here. Sandwiches are huge." Molly tapped the top of Hugh's menu. "Last time we were here Charlie had the pulled pork. His moans of pleasure bordered on obscene."

Ivy added, "One time I had Bobby's special ham and turkey club for lunch *and* supper, and there was still a bit left for the next day."

Jack cut in, mischief in his face and voice. "You *had* the club, Ivy? Don't you mean you tasted it? Or experienced it? Or perhaps savored it?"

Ivy ignored him. She tasted her ale and sighed extravagantly. "Oh, yum. I don't think I've ever had anything quite this supremely delicious."

"*Had* again?! I thought you had sworn an oath never to use that word."

She took another swig and licked the foam off her upper lip.

"As I've said before, Jack, *have, had, having* are all perfectly fine words—and very appropriate for use with inanimate objects. Like this very good ale."

Jack snorted and stood up, digging a cell phone out of his pocket. "Well, no matter how good the nachos look when they come, I don't want anyone to HAVE any of my portion before I get back. I'm going to check in with my wife."

"What was that about?" Hugh was watching Jack walk toward the front room.

"Jack and I have different birding styles."

Molly laughed her startling whinny. "And he loves riding her about it."

"What does it have to do with *had*?"

"Jack, like many birders, uses words like 'get' and 'had'. I got an Olive-sided Flycatcher today. I had forty species yesterday." She watched Hugh take a long swallow of ale. "Do you like it?"

"It's very good."

Molly leaned forward. "Ivy told Jack that people go *get* a dozen eggs. Or they *have* the tuna melt for lunch. But they should *see* or *watch* living creatures."

"I'm missing the point."

"You've been on only three of my walks now. But you can see that I like to amble along. I like to enjoy whatever comes our way. If we see something fascinating, like that Great Blue Heron balancing on the top of that tree, I like to stop and watch. Jack sometimes feels that looking at the same bird, especially a relatively common bird, for even five minutes is a waste of time when we could be 'getting' other species."

Ivy stopped for another sip, and Molly continued. "So Jack's Sunday outings focus on numbers, on getting to see the largest number of species. He makes a list of what's been seen recently, and where, and everyone drives around all over the place looking for those birds. Ivy calls it shopping cart birding."

"But here comes Jack, and I like Jack, and I don't want to rehash this with Jack, so let's change the subject."

Jack was accompanied by Bobby and the waitress, both of whom carried huge trays of appetizers. The entire table, except Hugh and young Sean, burst into song, in several different keys but with unanimous volume and enthusiasm.

"Food! Glooooorious food! OUR FAV-OR-ITE DI-ET!"

Ivy grinned at Hugh. "Another BBC tradition."

"From *Oliver*."

She raised her eyebrows.

Hugh moved back a little so the waitress could set a platter of potato skins on the table. Then his red-brown eyes flicked to Ivy's face. "Why would my knowing a piece of music surprise you? You barely know me."

Ivy gingerly picked up a hot potato skin and started winding the stringy cheese around it. "You're right. For all I know, you could be the NY Times critic for Broadway musicals."

"I'm not. I'm an architect."

Jack picked up his glass and rapped it with a fork. "Announcement!" He cleared his throat and looked up and down the table, his eyes sparkling. "The wife and I can make it official. She is the wife plus one. We're expecting our first child in just five short months."

All along the table, the birders called out congratulations. Molly lifted her glass. "To the proud papa, the incubating mama, and the soon-to-be chick."

"Thank you, thank you. Refills on the house. On me, actually. You all pick your designated drivers."

Ivy put her hand over the top of her glass. "I get icky-feeling after more than one. I can drive someone's car."

Hugh leaned closer. "All right with a stick?"

"Beg pardon?"

"A stick shift. Can you drive my Audi?"

"Sure."

He lifted his glass. "I don't party."

Ivy felt Molly nudge her leg under the table and carefully avoided looking toward her.

"So I rarely drink. But this is very good. I might have a second. You should drive."

She nodded. "Okay."

Halfway down the table, Charlie spoke up, his voice unusually deep and gloomy. "I'll drive. I'm not drinking."

Jack stared, astonished and aghast. "Not drinking? Not drinking Bobby's best? MY best?" He rose halfway out of his chair and leaned across the table, staring down at Charlie's glass. "Wait a goldarn sec here! Is that ROOT beer?"

The older man sent a sideways look at his grandson, and Sean let out a triumphant hoot. "We had a bet! When you said we might see a Black Tern when we were driving, my Grampa said it was too early. But I looked up the earliest day they get back to Vermont and it's right around now. So we made a bet. If Grampa was right and we didn't see a tern, I had to weed his garden."

"That's all?!" Jack was indignant. "But because we did see a Black Tern and you won a measly bet, poor

Charlie here has to suffer a great, staggering, catastrophic loss? Lunch at Bobby's without Chubby Sturgeon ale!"

Sean's grin widened. "Yup. If he lost, he had to be a kid for lunch."

Charlie nodded glumly. "Root beer." He wiped the foam off his enormous mustache and let out a gusty sigh.

****

In the back seat of Hugh's car, Molly stretched her arms over her head luxuriously. "A long walk, hours outdoors in the sun and wind—*always* good for body and soul—and now everyone's full of food and camaraderie and bird memories."

"And alcohol." Hugh tipped his head back onto the headrest. "Too much alcohol." He glanced over at Ivy. "Thank you for driving. Do you mind stopping at the park-and-ride first and switching to your car and then dropping me off at my house? I can walk down tomorrow and get the Audi."

"Sure."

"Don't forget to leave me at my daughter's, Ivy. That's between the park-and-ride and where Hugh lives."

"Got it, Moll."

****

Ivy glanced over at the silent man beside her.

"You'll have to direct me."

He groaned.

"My goodness, Hugh. How many glasses did you have?"

"Three. Maybe four." He rolled his head to look at her. "I'm not used to drinking. Alcohol is a social thing, and I haven't socialized for years. Take this left."

Late afternoon sun slanted through the trees as Ivy headed up into one of Montpelier's many hilly sections. The street was striped with the shadows of tall maples and oaks.

"You had fun today."

"Well, yeah, Hugh. Those people are my friends."

"Even Jack? He's a lot, um, noisier than you are."

Ivy grinned. "He is a bit bumptious. But he's a truly wonderful person. He's warm and sunny and humorous and energetic. And honest. He's very dear to me."

"But you don't go on his FATSO trips. Do you?"

She grimaced. "Rarely. I don't much like being trapped in a car for hours with people who love to talk. Loudly. And when they stop to 'get' a specific bird, every minute that they're not actually looking right at the bird, they do even more talking."

Ivy was silent for a moment, choosing her words. "Jack's style of birding is… it's convivial. Social. For Jack, and for many other people, social interactions are a huge part of birding. Birding is a way to meet people and spend time with people. But for me birding is mostly a way to spend quiet time in nature."

"So why don't you go birding alone?"

"I do. At least three times a week in spring, summer, and fall. Not quite so often in the winter." She slowed to let two children on bikes cross the street. "I lead a FATSO trip only one Sunday out of four, so the other Sundays are free. And Molly opens the shop for me one day a week so I have that morning too."

"Hang another left."

"And I often go for short bird walks really early, before work."

"Where?"

36

"Hubbard Park, usually."

"I never see you at the park. I'm there every morning."

"You're a runner, right? Runners usually stick to the cinder trails."

"Yes. I do."

"I take the cinder trail up the hill and then go on one of those little dirt woodland paths."

"That's a very lonely part of the park."

"Solo birding, Hugh. Alone."

"Take the next right."

Ivy turned onto a steeply sloping road with houses climbing the hills on both sides. The homes looked architect-designed, with large lots and expensive landscaping and little signs announcing which security company would come running at the first hint of an intruder.

"Second house on the left."

"Yikes. It looks wonderful."

The wood and glass house was set well back from the street, cantilevered over a steep ravine.

"My design." Hugh lifted his head from the headrest and stared at the house. "I designed our old house too. The one my ex-wife burned down." He leaned forward to pick up his pack from between his feet. His voice was muffled, and Ivy didn't hear his next words clearly.

"What?"

He sat up, holding the pack on his lap. He turned his head and spoke very precisely, as if he had to work to avoid slurring. "Sur-ro-gates. Our sur-ro-gate babies died in the fire. Not real ones. Not worth the hand clutched to the breast."

Ivy put her hand back on the steering wheel. "I

thought you said the fire killed the Sherpa babies."

"What on earth would Elaine and I be doing with Sherpa babies?"

"I don't kn—"

"We had surrogate children. I had a dog, a West Highland White Terrier. She had zebra finches." Hugh put his hand on the door handle and then turned back to Ivy. "My dog died, her finches got cooked, we lost the house, and it ended our marriage. It was quite a night."

He opened the door and got out of the car. Ivy watched him as he walked down the slanted walkway. He didn't stumble, so she decided it was all right to leave him alone.

Hugh MacDougal's house, even from the outside, was a revelation to Ivy. She had never in her life had what most people would consider normal living quarters. Until she was six years old, her bedroom was circular, twenty feet in diameter, and more than thirty feet high. Her grandparents spent most of their adult lives renovating an old barn with an attached silo but they didn't get around to splitting the silo into two stories until long after Ivy and her parents moved out.

After the silo, Ivy lived in a library.

****

"It's the only available house in town, Christine. The town library's downstairs, but that's irrelevant. The upstairs apartment is more than adequate for the two of us and Ivy. And I can't take this principalship if I have to commute sixty-four miles one way every single day. Not with school board meetings that last until late and supervisory duties at ball games and dances."

"What did you say about the will? A clause or something that could get us the place for free?"

"It's a codicil, Christine, not a clause. Back at the turn of the century, the builder willed this house to the town with the stipulation that the town library has to remain on the first floor. It's open only two afternoons and two evenings a week. We won't even notice it."

"But what about the librarian living upstairs?"

"I told you already, Christine. If the person who lives upstairs is also the librarian, she—it's always been a she—and her immediate family can live there rent-free. But if the town has to hire someone as the librarian, someone who lives elsewhere, then the people who stay in the apartment have to pay rent. That's eminently fair."

"Well, I want to do it. Be the town librarian."

"Don't be absurd, Christine. You don't know the least thing about running a library."

"You said they're not looking for a professional librarian."

"Of course they're not. No professional librarian would ever choose a rinkydink library in somebody's house. I told you. This whole century the librarian has been just somebody's wife."

"Well, then. I'm somebody's wife."

"Christine, I do not want to have this conversation. You have a full-time job being a principal's wife and mother to our daughter. And, I might add, at times that job stretches you to the limits of your capabilities."

The argument ended after her father figured out how much of his salary they could put into savings if he went along with her mother's cockamamie idea.

Ivy wouldn't have believed it when she was six years old, but living in a library almost made up for the pain of moving away from Grandmum and Pappap. For all the hours each week when the downstairs library was closed to the public, it was her own private hideaway and sanctuary, a place where she could be alone for hours as she read and dreamed and imagined.

"Ivy, you are spending far too much time downstairs."

"I'm reading, Mom. Reading is good. All the teachers say so."

"When I was in high school, I went to sleep-overs. And parties. And football games. And school dances. You're turning into a hermit."

"I am not a hermit, Mom. I spend seven hours a day with other people, in school. I even talk with them. I chat. I laugh. Just like a normal girl."

****

Then came college and a sprawling loft over a Portuguese fish market.

"Ivy, I'm not sure it's wise for you to share an apartment with three young men. Everyone will think you're a, a harlot."

"Almost the twenty-first century, Mom. No one will think I'm a harlot because no even knows that word." Ivy looked up from packing notebooks into a box, gazing at her mother with a thoughtful expression. "They might think I'm a slut, however."

"That is highly inappropriate language to use around your mother, Ivy."

Ivy kept talking. "But they would be wrong. All three of those young men, as you call them, are boys. I've known two of them since kindergarten. I still remember Clem peeing in the sandbox. Now they're into video games and *Star Wars* marathons and wearing their baseball caps backwards. My maidenhead is secure."

"Video games and movies are not the only things

young men think about, Ivy. You will be putting yourself in a highly vulnerable position, alone with the three of them."

"I disagree, Father. It's much safer with three than with just one. Anyway, they feel like my brothers. Younger brothers." She stood up. "Tell you what. If I end up pregnant or with some dreadful STD, you can stop paying your part of my tuition."

There was only one time when there was even a question of having sex with any of her roommates. And it was Clem. Beautiful Clem, with the beautiful long furry tanned legs that he showed off whenever possible by wearing shorts and sandals. Clem, who had always called her Dude until the weekend when it was just the two of them alone in the apartment.

"So, Ivy. Your bed or mine?"

"Beg pardon?"

"Tom and Ernest are gone all weekend, Ivy. This is our chance."

One time in the past year, Ivy had been surprised by a vivid fantasy about running her tongue over the intriguingly hairless skin on Clem's inner thighs. But she'd never once fantasized about kissing his mouth, about looking into his face in passion, about taking him into her body.

"Aw, come on, Clem. You know there are *so* many women on this campus who would be delighted to help you scratch whatever itch you're feeling. But not me."

"Why not?" He tucked in his chin and looked at her soulfully, his eyes huge. "Don't you loooove me?"

Ivy reached over and ruffled his hair. "Of course I love you. I have since we were tots. But we've got two more years together. Let's keep it simple. You're gorgeous—and you know it—but I'm not going to bed with you."

"Okay, dude. No biggie."

****

And then there was Professor Terhune and the commune.

Professor Terhune was only eight years older than Ivy but he was an adult, not a boy, with an adult job and adult interests and, for Ivy, adult allure.

"You're taking a class with Prof Terhune? Sit in the front! He might be small but he's a hunk. A pocket Adonis!"

Ivy thought the other young women were exaggerating but it turned out that Professor Terhune was, truly, an extraordinarily handsome man, even at five foot two.

"And check out his bulge. Our favorite prof might not be tiny all over, if you know what I mean."

Ivy had never before checked out a teacher's bulge. But she sat in the front of the class and she checked out his bulge and she started daydreaming about what it might be like with Prof Terhune, what it might feel like to have his small neat hands touch her, how kissing and making love would work given the difference in their heights, whether he might be muscular under his neat corduroy and wool, what the bulge in the front of his trousers might look like and feel like.

Three weeks before graduation, Professor Terhune asked her to stay after class. The question was so precisely in line with Ivy's daydreams that she was startled and embarrassed.

"Ivy, you may have heard that I'm taking a year-long sabbatical to study the remnants of commune culture in rural Vermont."

"Oh. No. I didn't know that. Communes?"

"Yes, indeed. This state has a long history with intentional cooperative communities. During the sixties, a greater percentage of people lived in communes in Vermont than in any other state. And, amazingly, several of those 1960s communes are still going."

"That's amazing. I had no idea."

"I'm going to need an assistant. It should take three to six months to get material for a book, and it would look good on your resume. I've arranged to stay at a good-sized commune that was formed in 1963. Asparagus Haven."

"Beg pardon?"

"That's the commune's name. Asparagus Haven. Many of the so-called hippie communes had intentionally whimsical names."

Two days after graduation, Ivy and the professor filled his car with boxes of clippings and notes and headed for the hills northeast of Montpelier. He drove without talking, intent on what Ivy was sure were deep and scholarly thoughts, leaving her to dream. The two of them would become a legend in the world of sociology. They would spend their lives together, working on study after study, book after book. Their relationship, their partnership, and eventually their marriage would inspire college students across the country.

"This is it, Ivy. We'll have to find Pete about where to stay. He's probably in the communal dining room."

Pete was a perfect match for Ivy's mental image of a communal farmer. His sturdy body was dressed in muddy jeans, plaid flannel, and a stained t-shirt. He wore sandals with wool socks. His hair was long and drawn back into a ponytail, and his face was weathered, with whitish squint lines around his eyes. He beamed when he saw the professor and rushed over to envelop the other man in a bear hug.

"This is Ivy, Pete. She's agreed to be my assistant for the project."

"Great to meet you." He turned back to the professor. "And great to see you, Mac. I can't tell you how great. There's just enough time to get you two situated before lunch."

He led the way to a one-story building that looked like a misshapen starfish, with short "legs" projecting in every direction.

"Your tree house will be ready in a week or two, but for now there's an empty room in here."

He pushed open a door into a small room with a toilet and sink in one corner, a dresser, a rocking chair, and a huge bed piled with colorful quilts.

"Will this do?"

Ivy looked at the bed and flushed. "Er. Yes. This looks excellent. Is it okay for y…?"

The men had already turned and were walking away. Through the open window, Ivy heard the professor's voice, rough and low and breathless, so different from the voice he used for lectures.

"I don't want to wait, Pete. Can we skip lunch?"

She watched as Pete, laughing, turned to the professor and pulled him close and they kissed, their bodies straining together, their hands restless and hungry.

The next morning, Professor Terhune, his hair uncombed and dressed in cut-off jeans and sandals, started interviewing the members of Asparagus Haven.

Ivy went to work making order from his boxes of notes, clippings, and files, and then moved on to transcribing and organizing interview data. In November, the day after the first snow fell, Professor Terhune thanked Ivy for helping him with what he called "a highly important book, possibly even a seminal book" and said that he and Pete would be leaving in the morning to continue sharing their lives and their dreams at a commune in the southern part of the state.

Ivy considered her options. Then she met with the Assembly of Equals and petitioned to be allowed to stay on at Asparagus Haven.

For the next dozen years, Ivy lived in a one-room tree house, climbing a ladder and pushing open a trapdoor, carrying a backpack full of wood up the ladder for her tiny cast iron stove, going down the ladder to use her own private outhouse with state-of-the-art worm composting technology, bathing sometimes in the showers beside the communal hot tubs and sometimes in cold water poured into a chipped white basin up in her tree house. She assisted the elderly herbalist, managed the commune's extensive lending library, and worked in the barns and gardens like every other member over the age of five. Her always-thin body toughened, got stronger. Her legs and arms and hands grew brown. Her blue eyes became startling in her tanned face. She let her dark curly hair grow and wore it in a thick braid that finally reached her waist.

Even with chores, Ivy had time to wander. The hay fields, orchards, and woodlots were full of wildlife. Orioles and bluebirds nested in the apple trees. Bobolinks and meadowlarks sang in the hilly fields that weren't mowed until mid-summer. The marsh around the swimming pond had herons and ducks, muskrats and otters. The woodlots were full of thrushes and warblers, and Ivy found the big messy nests of a Barred Owl and a Broad-winged Hawk.

Ivy imagined herself growing old at Asparagus Haven. Maybe she'd want to move from the tree house to something without a ladder by the time she reached seventy or so, but for now she loved her tiny home with its two windows and the miniscule woodstove that made it so cozy in the winter. It would be great, wonderful, amazing if some day there was an unattached man for her to love, who would love her. But she could imagine a happy life even if she remained alone. Maybe she would be lucky enough to die at Asparagus Haven, a peaceful death, surrounded by fresh air and bird song.

But a few days after she quietly celebrated her twelfth anniversary at the commune, Ivy got a message to call her father. Her mother had had a stroke.

Chapter Six

"She's in the second bedroom. She's expecting you."

At first, Ivy thought nothing had changed, that her mother had made an immediate and full recovery. Christine was sitting in an easy chair. Every hair was in place, as always. Her blouse was ironed and spotless, as always. Her cardigan was over her shoulders, held in place with a little chain.

But there was a football game on the TV. Her mother rarely watched television and never, ever watched sports.

"Mom?"

Christine muted the TV and turned her head. "Oh. Ivy." She stuck her legs straight out in front of her and looked at the brand-new white athletic shoes. "Not me, are they? I've never had sneakers in my life."

"Goodness." Ivy balanced on the edge of the bed. "Not even as a kid? How did you manage that?"

"Ministers' kids wore leather Mary Janes. Principals' wives wore leather pumps. And stockings." Christine flexed her feet. "My feet have hurt for thirty years, and now they don't. Yeah. It took having a stroke for me to be comfortable."

Yeah. Ivy couldn't remember ever hearing her mother use the word *yeah*. She would have thought it was evidence of a speech problem, but the rest of

Christine's words were as precise and clear as always.

"I just want to see this next play and then I'll turn it off. I got the DVD through interlibrary loan so I can keep it a few weeks."

Ivy waited, astonished, as her mother turned up the sound and leaned forward to stare at the TV.

"NY Giants vs. Redskins. 1962. Y.A. Tittle threw seven touchdown passes in that game."

"I never knew you liked football, Mom."

"Always. When I was in high school, I went to every game. All four years. After that I followed the Giants. Your father was no fan. I watched when he wasn't home." She snorted. "The principal's wife's secret vice. Here's one of the touchdowns.... Ahhh. That pass is poetry in motion."

Christine sighed, clicked the TV off and turned to face her daughter. And Ivy saw that it wasn't just the football game and the sneakers. Her mother's eyes were different. Her face didn't look distorted, as Ivy had feared, but the expression in her eyes was completely unfamiliar.

"Y.A. Tittle was the first pro football player to make the cover of *Sports Illustrated*. I bought that issue. And many others." She snorted again. "I kept them under the mattress. Like a girl with a secret diary. There's your dad, sleeping in the bed with me, never knowing we're sharing the bed with Y.A. Tittle, Joe Namath, and little Doug Flutie." She pulled her sweater closer around her shoulders. "Little compared to other football players, anyway. So. How long are you here for?"

"I'll stay as long as you need me."

"Oh no, don't say that." Christine put both hands on the arms of the chair and started pushing herself upright.

"You'll give up your whole life, the way I did."

Ivy moved toward her mother but Christine waved her off. "I had a few uses to start with. Cooking, cleaning, buying groceries. Sex. Rarely. And before your father retired, I would sit next to him at school functions. Dressed like the principal's wife. Smiling like the principal's wife."

She got to her feet and stood for a moment as if making sure she was stable.

"And the work in the library, Mom."

"Ah, yes. Saved us a bundle. Hence the only worthwhile thing I've ever done." Christine took a step, breathed deeply, and then took another. "But now I have no purpose at all. Your father will be only too happy to have you take my place. Let's have some coffee."

The kitchen was always Christine's domain. She alone knew where everything was. She did all the cooking. She alone put the dishes in the dishwasher and then put the clean dishes away. Now she simply sat down and waited for Ivy to find things.

"So. Ivy. What kept you there?"

"Beg pardon?"

"At that commune. What kept you there so long? Was it a specific person? A man?"

"No. Not a man."

"A woman?"

"No."

Ivy looked up from pouring coffee. Her mother's normal expression had always been one of mild interest and vague concern. Now Christine didn't look vague at all. Her eyes were sharp, measuring, a bit cold.

"Actually, Mom, it *is* a woman that keeps me there. It's me. I've stayed at Asparagus Haven, I love staying at Asparagus Haven, because I'm me there."

Ivy was startled to see her mother's eyes suddenly blaze with anger. She couldn't remember ever having seen anger on her mother's face, not ever. She kept talking, feeling absurdly like a defiant teenager.

"I'm not the principal's daughter, I'm not the teacher's pet, I'm not the slightly-too-tall and definitely awkward loner. I'm not a weirdo. I'm just wonderfully, gloriously, me."

"Push that chair closer."

"What?"

"The chair. I want to put my feet up."

Ivy put one of the kitchen chairs in front of her mother and watched as she lifted her legs with her hands and propped both feet up.

"I've never put my feet on furniture in my life." She flexed her ankles and glared up at her daughter. "I've also never felt like me."

"I'm... I'm sorry."

"You should feel sorry. I wouldn't have stayed with your father if I hadn't been pregnant. But I guess you didn't ask to be conceived. Cookies are in the cabinet to the left of the sink."

Ivy felt as if she was one or two steps behind her mother's train of thought.

"Pardon?"

"Cookies. Left of the sink."

When Ivy reached up to open the cabinet door, she saw that her hand was shaking. She didn't know the cold-eyed woman at the kitchen table, didn't know how to talk with her, didn't know how to find the mild, unthreatening, distant mother she'd known all her life.

"You were a cute baby, Ivy. But you represented a

great big door clanging shut between me and a possible real life. With a frigging huge padlock on it. No. Get the ginger ones."

In silence, Ivy carried the box of cookies to the table and then the two mugs of coffee.

Christine picked up her mug with both hands, brought it close to her face and sniffed. "French Roast. Your father's favorite. I prefer medium roast." She took a sip. "The doctor said I could have another stroke anytime now."

Ivy sat and opened the cookie box.

"Decades of drinking coffee I don't really like and wearing shoes that hurt my feet and watching football in secret. Every single day acting. Pretending. Never once talking to one single person in my own voice."

Ivy's hand jerked when her mother gave a sudden harsh laugh.

"I should have been the one to run away to a commune, Ivy. Wouldn't that have been funny? If I'd run away leaving you with your father and then years later we'd met up by accident in your commune?"

"What are you girls talking about?" Ivy's father came into the kitchen and headed for the coffee pot.

"I was just getting ready to tell our daughter that I hope she experiences more love in her life than I have. And more sex."

For a split second, Mr. Pritchard stopped as if he'd run into a glass wall. But he recovered almost immediately, addressing himself to Ivy as he filled his mug.

"I apologize for your mother, Ivy. One of the brochures from the doctor mentioned that stroke victims often take a long time to be themselves again. Their memories are often inaccurate. And they can suffer a lack of inhibition."

Ivy slowly moved her eyes from her mother's face to her father. "I agree that Mother might be feeling uninhibited. But I think her memories are clear. And I think she's very much herself."

****

Ivy's mother had only five weeks out of her whole adult life to be herself, to say what she was thinking, to drink the medium roast coffee Ivy bought for her, to prop her feet up on the furniture while she was reading the latest issue of *Sports Illustrated* or watching football on TV.

The second stroke happened as she and Ivy were making potato salad. Christine made a sudden throaty noise, and Ivy looked up to see the two sides of her mother's face going in two different directions. Christine's right eye was wide and frightened, the right side of her mouth struggling to open wide, to scream. The left corner of her mouth was being pulled toward her suddenly drooping eye, the left cheek bulging and throbbing. Christine started to reach up and touch her face, and Ivy lunged forward and grabbed the paring knife out of her hand and yelled for her father.

It took just a few seconds, a few seconds when blood wasn't flowing through a small vessel in her brain, for Christine to lose her speech. The last words Ivy ever heard her mother say were "Miracle Whip is too sweet for potat…"

This time, while her mother was still in the hospital, Ivy drove to Asparagus Haven and cleaned out her tree house. Then she walked to the beaver pond and sat on the remnants of an old dam to say goodbye.

The spring sun was warm on her head and back and she wanted to stay right where she was forever. She didn't want to smell hospital smells and talk again with nurses and physical therapists and watch her mother's face, waiting for the moment when Christine understood how much she had just lost.

A tiny bird appeared from nowhere, showing Ivy just a flash of its striped head and cinnamon-colored underside before it ducked into a hole near the top of a bare snag. It reappeared in seconds with a bill full of something that looked like rusty steel wool. Ivy could hear the little noise the nuthatch made as it spit out the rotting wood.

"Are you going to nest there, little nuthatch?" Ivy whispered.

She sat and watched as the bird removed mouthful after mouthful of rotten wood.

"I nested here too. I wish I could stay."

She hadn't known she was going to cry until she felt wetness on her hands. She bent her head and sobbed until she was finally able to take a deep breath, straighten up, and leave.

****

Ivy started calling her mother by her first name the day after the second stroke. "Mom" was the vague, distant woman from Ivy's childhood. Christine was the woman in the wheelchair, the woman with one eye that glowed with frustration or anger, with half a mouth that softened in a partial smile or twisted in sardonic amusement.

Ivy bought a notepad and three felt-tipped pens that made marks with very little pressure. Christine's first attempt required ten minutes for one sentence. After that, she limited herself to a few letters at a time. But conversations with her mother became the highlight of Ivy's days.

****

"My boss, Bill, knows diddlysquat about birds but he knows a lot about marketing. He read somewhere that birdwatching is the fastest-growing pastime in North America. There wasn't a single optics store for birders in the northern two-thirds of the state so he knew he'd have a near monopoly. Of course, a lot of people buy on-line. But it's good to be able to try binocs and scopes before buying so the store's doing really well. I've been picking up extra hours almost since I started."

—*good*—

"I met some members of the BBC today, Christine. No, not British television personalities. The Burlington Bird Club. I've been birding for years and years but I never even knew such a thing existed. One of the birders is a very enjoyable little woman. Her name's Molly. She looks like a fairy godmother, all twinkly and white-haired and cute. Bill wants me to join the Montpelier chapter of the BBC. No. It's the Montpelier branch of the Burlington Bird Club. Not a chapter but a branch, because of birds. Bill thinks we can wean local birders away from internet sales by making the store, in his words, the birdwatching hub of the whole state. He's thinking about regular bird walks or evening talks at the store or something."

—*good*—

"I came alarmingly close to making a complete fool of myself today, Christine."

The skin over her mother's right eye tightened, all that was left of a questioning frown.

"I'm not really attracted to Bill, my boss. I think I told you that. But recently I've been enjoying the way his back looks when he reaches up to put something on a top shelf. And how his chinos stretch across his butt."

—*norml*—

"Yes, I know it's normal. Propinquity. One male and one female, together all day every day. We eat scones out of the same tin. We take turns making coffee for each other." She looked out the window and took a deep breath. "So a few days ago I started daydreaming about a shared future, Christine. For the second time in my life. I was wrong the other time, too."

Her mother made a spasmodic movement, and Ivy covered her right hand with her own.

"A few weeks ago, Bill started talking about weddings. What do I think about the Trapp Family Lodge for a winter wedding? Do I have any ideas about destination weddings? Do I think it's fair to ask friends and relatives to spend a lot of money traveling long distances?

"He's never touched me. Except accidentally. Which makes what I was thinking particularly dumb. But I worked it all out in my mind. Just listen to this reasoning. Absurd! I figured that Bill is first and foremost a practical businessman, and he knows he's found a good thing in me, good for his store anyway, and so he decided to make me his life partner. As a practical decision." She took a deep breath. "I'm past thirty, Christine. A practical relationship might be the best I'm gonna get. Anyway, maybe… Maybe love and passion would come eventually."

Ivy felt her lips twist, almost like her mother's cynical little smile. "I know. I read too many romance novels."

—*me2*—

"Really? You used to read romance novels?"

—*secrt*—

"Dad didn't know, huh? *Sports Illustrated* and romance novels. You wicked woman."

—*hah*—

"I bet we can get romance novels as talking books. I'll get some for you so you don't have to struggle with turning the pages."

—*ok*—

"So—To get back to making a fool of myself. Almost. Today Bill asked me to stay late. He said he wanted to talk about something serious. He said it was time for us to move to the next level. Those were his exact words. Move to the next level."

Her mother's eye met hers steadily.

"And then he said he wants to make me a partner in the store." She looked down and gently rubbed her thumb over her mother's hand. "Because he's going to be there so much less."

Christine made a long grunt.

"Yeah. He wants to be home more often. He wants suppers with his girl. Movies and restaurant dates on Fridays. Maybe bowling."

Ivy shook her head.

"I'm sitting there, trying to process the, the whole bowling thing, and he gives me this huge doofy grin, reaches into his pocket, takes out a ring box, and tells me he's going to ask his girl to marry him. Lucky I was paying attention, huh? I could have seen that ring and burst out with yes, Bill, yes! That would have embarrassed both of us to death."

—*sory*—

"Yeah. Well, probably for the best. So, anyway, I'm going to start leading some bird walks, Christine. Somebody else already does one outing a month, so we'll have to coordinate." She wiped a bit of chocolate pudding from the side of her mother's mouth. "I haven't met that guy yet, but I was introduced to two more BBC members today. There's a serious looking woman, as tall as I am, Christine. I think she's vain about her hair. She wears it in a big bun at the back of her neck but it must go almost to her waist when she lets it down."

—*nice*—

"Yes." Ivy looked up and smiled at the orderly who came in to pick up Christine's dinner tray. "And there's an older guy with this huge blond mustache that droops down on both sides of his mouth all the way to his jaw."

—*vik*—

Christine made a sudden noise and her fingers whitened around the pen.

"Cramp?" Ivy wiggled the pen back and forth until she could slide it out of her mother's grasp. "You've been gripping that pen for ages this evening. We've been chatting too long."

Christine's brow moved and she glared.

"Okay. Not too long. You know I love chatting with you." She took her mother's hand in both of hers. "At least we know what it is this time. The first time you had a cramp scared me to death. I thought it was another… You did, too. But now we know exactly what to do."

It was quiet in the little room as Ivy slowly massaged her mother's hand.

"Getting better?"

Christine almost closed her good eye and then

opened it again.

"Good. So… What were you saying? Vick? Vike? Oh!" She beamed at her mother. "Viking! Yes! Charlie looks exactly like my mental picture of a Viking." She laughed. "Now that's all I'm going to think every time I see him! His big yellowish mustache and a helmet with horns."

****

The solarium was empty except for Ivy, her mother, and a huge ficus tree.

"Christine, I have something to discuss with you."

Her mother looked past Ivy and grunted.

"Will you look at me?"

Christine grunted again and flapped her right hand. She was staring fixedly out the window with her one good eye.

Ivy turned and saw a hummingbird only a few inches from the glass.

"Oh!"

She took her mother's hand and they watched the tiny bird as it darted from bloom to bloom in a hanging pot of fuchsia, hovering briefly at each flower, its throat sometimes black and sometimes flashing scarlet. After a few moments, the hummingbird moved down, out of sight until Ivy pushed her mother's wheelchair right up to the big window and they could look down at the bird feeding from bright red bee balm. They watched until the hummingbird flew out of sight, heading around the corner of the building.

"A little jewel. Thank you for pointing it out to me, Christine." She touched her lips to her mother's hand. "Okay. Here's the thing we have to talk about."

Her mother's eye met Ivy's steadily.

"Bill and his fiancée are going to move to Keene New Hampshire, so she can be near her family. He wants me to run the store, with him as silent partner."

Christine's right eyebrow lifted a few millimeters.

"I'd have to hire someone. I've been thinking of Molly from the BBC. Remember I told you about her? Tiny? Bouncy? White hair? She's come on two bird walks now and I like her. I think she retired a while ago so maybe she's ready for something part-time."

She looked intently at her mother.

"But it will mean many more hours at the shop and less time here with you. The mall doesn't open until ten, so I'll still be here in the mornings. And after closing, for an hour or so. And I'll still make some casseroles and stuff for dad, on Sundays. What do you think? Are you upset? Be honest with me."

—*good for u*—

"One problem with writing, Christine, is that I can't tell if it's sarcastic or not. Is that sarcastic? Are you saying 'well, whoopee for you, you bitchy daughter, go off and leave me alone and bored in this hellhole?' Tell me."

The right side of Christine's mouth twitched up. She picked up the pen again and made a quick slashing movement and then poked the paper hard with the felt tip. Ivy pulled the notepad closer.

—*good for u!*—

Vermont's famed leaf-peeping season was late that year. The sugar maples in front of the nursing home were still mostly green, but fall color was beginning to show in the hills and wetlands. Ivy decided to ask Christine if she'd like to be pushed around the block so they could look across the valley and see the trees on the ridgeline glowing in the sun.

"Christine?"

Ivy's mother was slumped sideways in her wheelchair, one arm hanging motionless, one hand touching the floor. Her hair, her always neat hair, had flopped forward and was hiding her face.

Ivy knew, even before she touched her, that Christine was dead. She knew she should call a nurse but instead she sat down on the floor next to the wheelchair and lifted her mother's cold hand off the floor. She held it between her own, stroking, caressing, wanting to share her own warmth.

After a long time, her eyes focused on one of the felt-tipped pens on the floor a foot or so from Christine's limp hand. Ivy raised her head. The notepad was on her mother's lap, caught between her torso and her thighs.

Ivy got to her knees and pulled the notepad toward her with both hands.

Dark lettering trailed unevenly across the page, becoming fainter near the right edge.

—*lov u I V*—

Chapter Seven

For a full week, the southwest and central plains were lashed by violent storms. Rain whipped the dry flat land, driven by winds that blew the roofs off shopping malls and tipped mobile homes onto their sides. Claps of thunder shattered plate-glass windows. The sky lit up with almost continuous lightning. The warbler joined thousands of other migrating birds, all buffeted and blown off course, all pushed north and east faster than they could fly, all trying only to keep breathing.

The warbler managed to land on the tallest thing for miles around, the only thing that even faintly resembled a tree. The old windmill had long ago rusted to immobility, its blades weathered into thin and twisted skeletons. The bird hopped around on what was left of the windmill blades, ducking its head and looking under in a futile search for juicy caterpillars. When the wind started again, it took shelter on the inside of the tall legs. A movement caught its eye. The thing didn't look like a caterpillar, but it was moving. The warbler lunged forward and caught the spider. Then another. And another.

There was nothing to keep the warbler where it was, nothing of the habitat it needed to find a mate and rear a nest full of youngsters.

It spread its gray wings and again flew north-north-east. Now there were cities and rolling farmland below but also, here and there, isolated patches of woodland. The bird left the sky each dawn and spent each day feeding, gobbling caterpillars, replacing the fat reserves that were almost gone.

And every place the bird stopped, it sang. It stood at the top of a tree, stretched its body to its fullest, threw back its head and caroled out the courtship song of its species. But no other Grace's Warbler ever answered.

At last, the warbler arrived at a place full of tall trees and peace. No wild wind buffeted the little bird or forced it to fly. No groups of picnickers ran and yelled below. No machine noises interrupted the stillness. A dog barked, but it was far away and of no interest. The long-needled trees were different from the piñons where the bird had started life, but they were full of caterpillars. The warbler no longer felt the need to migrate. It located two areas of tall pines for feeding. It found a place to roost at night, secure and protected. Alone, it settled into a new life.

Chapter Eight

Sharp-eyed Sean was the first Vermonter to see the rarity. "What's that bird?" The boy's hushed voice carried easily to the back of the Charlie's canoe. "Straight ahead of us, on that crooked branch hanging over the water... Darn. It flew."

"What'd it look like?"

"Little. Maybe a warbler? Or a vireo? I think..." Sean laid his paddle across the boat in front of him so he could use both hands for his binoculars. "There! Same branch again."

"Details, Sean. What tree?"

"With long needles. The..." Sean lowered his binoculars and scanned the area ahead of him. "Okay. It's the only tree in front of us with long needles."

"White pine."

"White pine. Um. Left side. The branch that's hanging over the water."

Charlie lifted his binoculars. "Got your bird. Looks gray. See anything else?"

Sean made a little humming noise as he watched the bird. "Yellow throat, I think. Yes."

"Belly color?"

"It's all yellow on its throat and chest and then white way down on its belly."

They watched the little bird as it moved out toward the end of the pine branch, picking at the base of the needles, occasionally leaning almost parallel to the water as it gleaned for insects on the underside of the branch.

"Back is gray. I see yellow on its face. Above its eye. Mmmmm. Oh! Below its eye too. Shit. I mean, drat! There it goes." Sean dug out his field guide. "Where should I look, Grampa?"

"Try warblers." Charlie's soft chuckle was a surprise. "This is it. What birding's all about."

"Being stumped?"

"Having to think about possibilities. Sean, tell me the possibilities. Warblers with gray backs, yellow throats, and yellow breasts."

"Well, Magnolia's got a yellow throat. And yellow on the breast. Nope… black stripes in the yellow. We couldn't have missed that, could we?"

"Magnolia female?"

"Well, maybe. No. This guy here's got yellow around his eye. Uh… There's Cape May. It's got a yellow throat." Sean's voice was hushed. "Nope. It's got some rusty stuff on its face. Ummm. Prairie Warbler? Nope. They've got stripes too. Hey! Grace's Warbler! It… Nope. They're in the southwest."

"Lemme see. Huh."

"If it's a Grace's Warbler, grampa, why would it be way up here?"

Charlie was still staring down at the book. His voice, when he answered, was distracted.

"Blown off course. Bad wiring in its brain. Dunno for sure." He closed the field guide with a snap and cleared his throat. "Well. Going out on a limb. Gonna report a Grace's Warbler. Gray back, nape and top of head. Yellow throat and breast. White wing bars. Lotsa yellow above the eye, little bit below the eye. White belly and undertail coverts."

He started turning the canoe. "No photo, so it's not going to stand. But it'll get people out here looking."

That evening, the rare warbler was seen by five more people, two from a rowboat and the others from an old logging road that looped around the end of the reservoir. The next morning, a kayaker got a clear enough photo to confirm the sighting. The bird was not only the first Grace's Warbler ever recorded in Vermont, but the first ever recorded east of the Mississippi.

By the afternoon after the first sighting, the parking lot at the reservoir was full. Several cars had out-of-state plates, the owners alerted to the rarity by e-mails from friends or postings on rare bird alerts. Most of the birders walked down the old logging road but some risked driving, inching their cars through gullies and up and over tree roots and around small boulders. A clearing at the north end of the reservoir became an unofficial second parking lot, soon clogged with cars and tripods and spotting scopes and birders. Many people carried cameras with huge lenses. A trio of birders from Massachusetts came prepared to spend the night, with a cooler and sleeping bags in the open back of their station wagon.

The warbler was seen five more times that day and six times on Sunday, always far up in the forest canopy. People grumbled about getting "warbler neck" and joked that there should be an on-site chiropractor.

By the end of the first week, the Grace's Warbler seemed to have established a routine. It spent part of each morning gleaning in the white pines at the northern end of the reservoir, left for several hours, and then returned again in late afternoon to the trees above the logging trail.

****

As Ivy got out of her car, a heavy motorcycle sputtered to a stop in the main parking lot and the lead rider called out the standard question: "Is it still here?"

The two men on the bike looked young, filthy, tired, and happy. "We're hoping to get the warbler and then head over to New York State for the ptarmigan, if it's still there. Then through Pennsylvania to get a Henslow's Sparrow. That one's not as rare but it'll be new for us."

The second rider climbed off the bike and stretched. "Three lifers, two thousand miles. Best vacation ever!"

Ivy squinted at the mud-covered license plate. "Where are you two from?"

"South Carolina."

"Yikes. You might take the prize for the longest trip to see our bird."

"Closer'n going to Arizona for it!"

Ivy walked with them to the end of the logging road and set up her scope. "The warbler was seen this morning. It usually comes back to this area around 3:30 or 4:00 p.m."

The two young men were like whippets, all nerves and energy, pacing back and forth in the clearing, turning this way and that, staring up and then straight ahead into the woods and then up again. Ivy saw the warbler and opened her mouth to say so, but both young men were already focused on it.

"Gray back."

"Check."

"Gray nape and crown."

"Yup."

"Yellow throat and belly."

"Checko!"

"White wing bars."

"Very check!"

"Yellow above the eye."

"Check that too."

"Yellow crescent under the eye? Can you pick it out?"

"Yes."

They turned to each other, smacked palms together in an exuberant high five, and then grinned at Ivy.

"Got it! Time to move."

They turned as one and ran back along the logging road with the grace and energy of youth.

"Twitchers," Ivy muttered.

"What?"

Ivy jumped. Hugh MacDougal was standing in the shadow only a few feet from her.

"Oh! I didn't see you." She turned back to the bird. "Those two. They're twitchers."

Hugh moved to stand next to her. "Again. What?"

"It's a British expression. It means someone who travels long distances to check off rare birds that are reported by other birders."

They stood silently watching the warbler. Often, when Ivy was watching one specific bird, she had the whimsical thought that she and the bird were alone together in a cone of quiet, separated from the rest of the world by her own intense watching and the bird's intense focus on survival. Now she was grateful that Hugh was silent, that he stood beside her without the constant conversation that most members of the BBC felt was essential for enjoyable birding.

She studied the warbler's movements as it gleaned,

the way it tipped its head to examine the underside of the thin branches, the way it sometimes hopped from one cluster of pine needles to another and sometimes fluttered.

After many minutes, they heard other birders approaching along the logging trail. The group made a noisy entrance into the clearing, and several found the warbler immediately and pointed it out to the others.

There was no real reason to whisper, with so much noise in the clearing and the bird so far away and so far above them, but Hugh's deep voice was barely audible. "How many times have you seen him?"

"Three, now. No. Four."

"Same here. What keeps us coming back?"

She turned her head slowly and looked at him. "Well, Beck says it's ghoulish fascination. We all want to know exactly when the bird disappears. How long it can last in a place that's so alien, so far from where it's supposed to be."

"I don't agree."

"Me neither."

They were quiet again, training their binoculars on the Grace's Warbler as it continued to do the only tasks that mattered: finding food, eating, staying alive.

Ivy turned back to Hugh. "I think there are two reasons. First, we all know—and we don't usually know when we're watching birds—that it's the same individual, that we're seeing the exact same bird we saw last time."

"Makes it personal."

"Yes… And, second, it's… I think some of us, anyway, keep coming back because we're touched. Vagrants like that little warbler will never get back to other members of their species. He's completely alone."

Hugh lowered his binoculars and looked at her. "And that speaks to you."

For the past twenty years, Ivy had always responded defensively when anyone commented on her solitude or suggested that she might be lonely.

"Yes."

"Same here."

Chapter Nine

After several days of gorging on fat caterpillars, sipping water from tiny pools on a high granite ledge and preening travel-worn feathers, the yellow and gray bird began again to sing the courtship and territorial song of its species.

No other male challenged it. No little female fluttered closer. No other Grace's Warbler answered the high, rapid, ascending song.

Chapter Ten

Two big maples stood at the top of the rise, one on each end of a small walled-in area with several mossy gravestones. Through the spotting scopes, the birders could see down into an old silo that had partially collapsed, making a concave platform for a big messy nest of sticks.

Jack's voice was uncharacteristically hushed. "Here comes mama. Or papa."

"And here comes papa! Or mama."

"What is… Looks like a dead rabbit."

"Man. Whatever it is, that big bill is turning it into stew meat wicked fast."

The Bald Eagle was tearing off chunks of flesh and bending to lay them in the nest.

"I thought they put the food right in the babies' mouths."

"They do, Sean. When the chicks are little fluffy white things. Now it's time for the babies to do at least some of the work."

"This is the coolest thing I've ever seen in my whole entire life."

"Even cooler than discovering a Vermont rarity?

"Oh. Well, maybe not, Grampa. But it's still awesomely cool."

"It is indeed."

****

The group approached the parking lot in an animated cluster, with Jack almost dancing with amusement. "And Charlie, with a completely straight face, told the guy he'd recognize a Western Sandpiper because it'd have a…" He struggled to get to the end of the story before he dissolved in laughter. "… a Pecos Bill!"

Molly whooped into her characteristic laugh but then stopped as abruptly as if she'd flipped a switch. "Heads up. The moody Scot."

Hugh MacDougal was alone at the edge of the parking lot, his lean body propped against his car. Even from a distance, he looked grouchier and more distant than usual.

Ivy waved and called to him across the lot. "Hi there! Are you waiting to find out what we saw before you head out?"

Beck's weathered face was uncharacteristically animated. "It has been a thrilling morning, Hugh. There are two eaglets. We watched the adult birds feeding them."

Hugh eyed Ivy coldly. "I got to the park-and-ride at eight. You had all left."

"Well yes. The meeting time was seven."

Ivy was suddenly uncomfortably aware of her mud-spattered trousers and sweaty hair. She felt herself getting defensive, and that made her irritated. "It's our standard, Hugh. It's on the website. We meet at nine o'clock November through February, eight o'clock in March and April, seven o'clock May through October. You were on time for the last trip, and that was at seven."

"I thought that one was earlier because it was a long drive."

Ivy moved a bit off the trail so the others could get to their cars. "Want me to tell you how to find the nest?"

"Forget it. I should have noticed about the starting time."

"You're here, ready for a walk. And it's not hard to find."

There was a pause, then he turned his whole body to face her. "Is it visible through binoculars? Or does one need a scope?"

"You won't see much with just binocs. Why don't you borrow my scope and tripod? You can bring them by the store tomorrow."

Hugh's head jerked back and he glared as if she'd just said something offensive. "That seems foolish. Giving your expensive scope to someone you hardly know."

"For Pete's sake. I do know you, Hugh! And I know where you live. I have no qualms whatsoever about letting you borrow my scope." She tapped her foot impatiently. "You haven't answered my questions. Do you want to see the eagle nest? Do you want directions?"

He held up one thumb. "I want to see the nest." He raised his index finger. "I don't want to borrow your scope." He raised his middle finger. "It sounds like there's no point in going without a scope." He folded his fingers into a fist, the knuckles white against his tan. "So no."

"For Pete's sake." She pulled her water bottle out of the side pocket of her vest and took a long drink. "Do you have any water with you?"

"What?"

"Water. Or food?" She beeped her car open and retrieved a second water bottle from the back seat. "I've

73

got two energy bars, an apple, and some gorp. If you've got anything, bring it along."

"You're making even less sense than I think might be usual for you."

"There's an eagle nest, with chicks. You want to see an eagle nest. I like showing eagles and nests and chicks to other birders. I'm going to take you to see it. Get your act together."

She started back along the trail without checking to see if he was following. After a while, she could hear his footsteps behind her.

"I'm taking the scope." He lifted the heavy tripod off her shoulder.

"Thanks."

Sun sparkled off muddy water. An intermittent south wind bent the cattails and the stands of flowering rush. They could hear the cries of gulls following a manure spreader more than a mile away. Quiet forest on one side, quiet fields on the other, and the quiet man behind her.

No chatter, no conversation. The thought came to Ivy that the best friends might not always make the best birding companions, and vice versa.

"Let's stop here for a snack, in the shade."

Hugh reached into one of the deep pockets of his pants and pulled out a Ziploc bag. "Cashews?"

"Thanks." She took several nuts and handed him an energy bar. "So what were you doing, between when you got here and when we all appeared?"

"I took a walk. I went the other way, into the woods instead of alongside the field."

"Did you see anything good?"

He shot her a look under his brows. "To quote you—

They're all good."

Ivy grinned. "Okay. What did you see?"

"A Hairy Woodpecker. Chickadees. Robins. Heard a vireo. Red-eyed I think. I'm pretty sure. Ovenbirds. Red-winged Blackbirds out in the grasses at the start, of course. Turkey Vulture went over my head."

She took a bite of her energy bar and chewed. "One time I foolishly tried wading across that big wet area on the far side of the parking lot." She grimaced. "I got slimed to the knees with the most foul-smelling muck, and then I slipped and fell down."

She thought he looked somewhat amused.

"And when I looked up, there were five vultures, circling, right above my head."

One corner of his mouth twisted up. "Waiting."

"Yup. To see how dead I was."

They stood quiet, chewing.

Ivy held out her hand. "Wrapper?"

"What? Oh." He handed her the paper from his energy bar, and she wadded it up with hers and tucked them into the back pocket of her vest.

"Okay. Let's go ogle eagles."

Hugh didn't move. He was looking into the distance, his face tense. "Before we go any farther, I need to say something."

"Okay."

"You're female."

"Good eye."

"And you're walking in a fairly remote location with a man you barely know."

"True."

"I just want you to know that there's no danger."

"I didn't think there was."

He glanced at her. "That's quite foolish. Bad things happen to women all the time."

She patted one of her vest pockets. "I have pepper spray."

"Oh. Good. But I want to finish what I started to say."

"Okay."

"I haven't been interested in sex for many years now. For you, this is just as safe as walking with another woman."

Ivy nodded briskly. "No rape today. Good to know." She raised her eyebrows and tilted her head, considering him. "But you could be some sort of crazed birder assassin with plans to kill me and, I don't know, use my skull for a wren house or something."

The expression on his face didn't change. "There's something else. I understand that you're single. Is that right?"

"Right."

"There can be a lot of societal pressure on single people. Especially single women. It occurs to me that you might be thinking of this as a, um, a date. I don't want you to think that. It's not."

Ivy leaned her back against the maple tree's trunk. "Anything else I should know?"

The man hesitated for a long moment. Then, "No. That's all." He held out the bag of nuts again and shook some into her hand. "Except a skull has too many openings for a wren house."

****

Hugh stood motionless, hunched over Ivy's scope, until the adult eagle left the nest. Then he straightened slowly. "Excellent, to use your favorite word. Thank you."

"My pleasure. Ready to go?"

He nodded and started zipping the cover around her scope.

"I can carry that now."

"So can I."

Neither of them talked again until they'd reached the parking lot. Then he turned to her and spoke formally, as if he'd been practicing what to say. "That was very exciting, Ivy. Thank you for taking the time to show me the Bald Eagle nest."

"I'm glad you enjoyed yourself." She turned toward her car. She got her shoes and socks out of her car and sat down on a thick log. "I think Mother Nature put this log here for this exact purpose, so hikers and birders can change out of their mud boots."

Hugh sat down beside her. "The logs were placed here to prevent incremental encroachment of the parking lot into the adjacent field."

"Whimsy isn't exactly your thing, is it?"

He pulled off his right boot and turned it upside down, letting a stream of water splash onto the ground.

"Jeez, Hugh, why didn't you say something? We could have come back the way we went instead of trudging through slop."

Hugh pulled off his socks. "I didn't know the boot had a hole in it until we'd already come a long way. It would have been foolish to turn back." He pushed up his right pant leg and started wiping his foot with the dry left sock. "Anyway, I don't melt when I get wet."

Above his ankle, on the inside of his leg, the skin was raised, shiny, and almost purple. The scarred area extended up under his pants.

"Were you injured when your house burned?"

His hand jerked. "How did you…?

"You mentioned the fire the night I drove you home."

"I… I obviously said way too much. I apologize."

"No need to apologize. You were tipsy." She was uncomfortably aware that he didn't move, that he sat frozen, while she tied her shoes.

"I have never talked about it. Not to anyone."

"Oh."

"My ex-wife left a candle burning in the bathroom. So it was her fault that it started. But she was home. She could have called 911. We could have had minor damage. But she didn't even notice the smoke alarms. And that was my fault."

"Why…?"

He cut her off. "Don't ask questions. I want to talk about this. This once. Never again." He took a deep breath and looked into the distance. "My wife never liked sex."

Ivy blinked.

"I thought she'd become more eager in time but she never did."

"Hugh, I think you're going to regret telling me this."

"I said something about surrogate children, didn't I?"

"Yes."

"That's why we needed them. Elaine didn't like sex and she didn't want children. Everyone else in the neighborhood had kids. We had zebra finches and a terrier."

Ivy was startled to see a partial smile, his teeth very

78

white under the red-brown of his moustache.

"Wonderful little animal. West Highland White Terrier. I always thought I didn't like little dogs but Elaine didn't want a big one. And Laird turned out to be intelligent and enjoyable. And loyal. He always came with me on my runs. One morning a man approached me for money and got belligerent when I said I didn't have any with me. Laird got right between the two of us, snarling and baring his teeth. It should have been comical for a dog his size, but it wasn't. It was clear that he was ready to defend me."

"It sounds like you were lucky to have had Laird in your life."

Hugh's eyes flicked to her face. "Lucky to have him? And then lose him?" He looked away again, his face tense and his eyes bleak. "I was driving home and I saw a glow in the sky. I started thinking about our neighbors. Wondering which family was losing its home. I never worried it could be our house. Not once. I never even worried about it until I got home and there were flames shooting out of the roof.

"I started yelling Elaine's name, running from fireman to fireman. Then I saw her next to one of the trucks. She wasn't crying until she saw me. Then she kept saying it was her fault, the fire was her fault, over and over. She said she could smell the birds burning." He shrugged. "I knew the birds didn't have a chance. But I thought I could hear Laird. My dog. I thought I could hear him howling. So I pushed Elaine out of the way and ran past the firemen. There was a lot of smoke but I couldn't see any flames so I kept running."

He closed his eyes for several seconds. Then he looked right at Ivy, his face twisted.

"I found Laird in the back hall. I thought he was breathing so I picked him up and turned to get out of the house. That's when the second story fell in."

Hugh turned away when she gasped.

"I don't remember anything else until the next day, in the hospital. Elaine was sitting by the bed. I asked her why she said the fire was her fault."

There was a long pause, and then Hugh forced the next words out through his teeth. "She was right there, when the fire started, while the fire grew and took the whole house and killed my dog. She was out in the gazebo. Having sex with my partner. The partner in my firm." His upper lip curled back over his teeth. "My frigid wife was having such passionate sex with someone other than her husband that she didn't even notice when every smoke alarm in the house went off."

Ivy wished she knew him better, so she could touch him and maybe change the expression in his eyes.

"Elaine… In the hospital… Elaine wouldn't stop talking. I didn't want to hear but she wouldn't stop talking. She told me she'd said no the first time. Said no repeatedly. But he wouldn't stop. He pushed her against a wall in the laundry room and wouldn't stop and she… She got excited. I was always so careful of her and he was rough and she got excited. He kept being rough, every time they met, and she kept on liking it.

"So. To the point of this saga. I hope, with all my being, that Elaine never stops feeling guilty for that fire. But I know, I can't escape knowing, that the real fault is mine. Our house burned to the ground, my dog died, and all her stupid zebra finches cooked, because I didn't give my wife what she wanted."

He shoved his feet into his shoes and stood up.

Ivy scrambled up from the log. "Wait. Is your… Is she still with your old partner?"

His face looked like a mask. No movement, no expression, waxy and still. A Great Crested Flycatcher made its loud wheeeep right above their heads but neither of them looked up.

Ivy was just about ready to concede the staring contest when the anger drained out of him, leaving him looking tired and sad. He flexed his fingers and cleared his throat. "They didn't last a month."

"And are you still in partnership with the traitorous swine?"

Hugh was startled into something like a laugh. "We're not partners any more. No. Thank you for calling him swine."

"Last question. How badly were you burned? How extensive are your scars?"

She thought he might balk but she also thought that his face had become more relaxed, calmer.

"Two different questions." He hesitated, twisting his mouth. "I was burned on my right leg and my left upper arm. The front and back of that shoulder. A bit on my chest. A little patch low on my back." He took a deep breath. "Those are the scars on my skin. Visible scars. They're negligible. They don't interfere with much."

He met her eyes.

"I don't mean to sound melodramatic. But there are other scars from that fire and they affect every aspect of my interactions with other humans. I don't believe they'll ever go away."

Chapter Eleven

Red-winged Blackbirds and Marsh Wrens flew to and from their nests in the cattails. Common Yellowthroats called "witchity witchity" from the low shrubs and grasses beside the water. Male Mallards and male Wood Ducks, like floating rainbows, patrolled the shoreline while their less showy mates hunkered down on grassy nests. An Osprey pair circled overhead, calling out warnings to the fishermen and kayakers below. In the thickets of saplings and sumac and dogwood, Yellow Warblers and Chestnut-sided Warblers added their spring sounds to the pure whistles and buzzy trills of Song Sparrows. An Eastern Wood-Pewee built its nest only a few yards from the vagrant's night roost. If the warbler had been interested, it could have watched the darker bird flying back and forth, bringing grass and spider webs to make the soft little cup, decorating the outside of the nest with chips of lichen until it was almost invisible on the horizontal branch.

The Grace's Warbler was the only bird in its new world that wasn't involved with territory, mating, and nesting.

Chapter Twelve

"I've been looking at a topo map."

Ivy looked up, startled. Hugh's long body was bending over the desk in the back room of her shop, and he was spreading out a map.

"You know when we're looking for the Grace's Warbler from the logging road, we can see a rock wall through the scopes, rising out of the woods, way in back?"

"Yes."

"Well, there's a sizeable ledge at the top of that cliff. You can't see it from the ground because it slopes back, but it's obvious on the map. I think it's possible to get up to that ledge and look *down* on the bird."

"Scale the cliff? Ropes and 'I'm on belay' and all that?"

He shot her an irritated look. "Don't be ridiculous. I'm talking about walking in a big arc from the logging road. I think you'd end up looking down into those tall pines, where the bird looks like it's heading whenever it leaves the logging trail."

Ivy leaned forward, her eyes beginning to sparkle. "So we might be able to watch the warbler without warbler neck."

"Precisely. Do you know if anyone has tried it? Walking up to the ledge?"

"That might be what that photographer did. The guy

from Quebec who got the awesome photos."

"Did he have any trouble? Denning bobcats? Landowners with shotguns?"

"Not that I heard."

"All right then." He rolled up the map and tapped it on the desk. "I'm going. Do you think any other members of the BBC might want to join me?"

"It's an off weekend for FATSO trips so normally everyone would be available, but I think a group is heading up to the eastern townships in Canada. Possible Upland Sandpiper, definite wine and cheese. But I'll send around an e-mail. When are you planning to go?"

"Tomorrow morning. Bright and early. The rain's supposed to end tonight."

"Carpool at seven, start walking at seven-thirty?"

"Perfect."

****

"Small group. We can all fit in my car."

Ivy and Charlie walked over to Hugh's Audi.

"Molly's babysitting her grandkids, and the Canadian expedition grew to ten people."

Charlie lowered himself into the front seat with a grunt. "Wasn't going to come this morning myself. Gardening injury."

"Beg pardon?"

"Tripped stepping out of one of the raised veggie beds. Twisted my ankle. Taped. It'll be fine."

The trail was muddy in places from the rain the day before but there were enough roots and fallen branches for fairly comfortable footing. Dew or rain sparkled on every leaf and every conifer needle and on gigantic spider webs woven from tree to tree to trap unwary flying insects. The air smelled clean and new, and there were late wildflowers hidden in many of the low areas below the trees. Ivy inhaled deeply and felt, as she so often felt in the woods, like one of the luckiest human beings on the whole earth.

****

"Hold up."

Hugh and Ivy turned to look at Charlie.

"I'm heading back."

"We don't have to walk this fast, Charlie. Let's stop and rest a while."

"Stopping. Resting. Walking slower. Won't help. Ankle's on fire. Hugh, give me your keys. I'll take a nap in the car."

Ivy glanced at Hugh and then back at Charlie. "Will you be all right? Walking back alone?"

He gave her an impatient look from under his bushy eyebrows. "Not ill, Ivy. Ankle hurts. And a coupla years older than you two mountain goats."

"Okay. Call if you want us to come back."

He turned to go, pulling a water bottle out of his pocket. "See you after you see the bird. Don't hurry. Enjoy it."

****

The ledge turned out to be bigger than either of them had expected, almost an acre of bedrock rising out of the meadow to jut high above the forest. Wherever there were hollows in the granite surface, there were rainwater pools and little gardens of sedge and wildflowers.

"I think we're right where you said we'd be, Hugh. I see something glinting that's probably sun on a car roof down in the main parking lot." Ivy dug out her cell phone. "Charlie? What's up?"

"Sean's mom's going to pick me up. Tell Hugh I'm

leaving the keys…" Ivy could hear rustling noises. "Big maple, imbedded barbed wire. Hanging the keys over the wire, back side of the tree."

Ivy put her phone away and cautiously joined Hugh near the edge. He glanced over at her.

"Do you have problems with heights?"

"Not severe problems." She took a step forward and craned her neck to look down an almost vertical rock wall dropping to the tops of tall trees and the forest floor below. "But I'm not going to stand here on the very edge and use binocs, that's for sure."

She sat down abruptly. "Much better." Ivy folded her legs and grinned up at him. "Tailor pose. Very stable."

Hugh lowered himself to the stone, raised both knees and leaned his elbows on them. In silence, they scanned the treetops.

"See that huge birch with the bare snag at the top?" Ivy was almost whispering. "Can't we see that through the scope, from below?"

"It looks different from this angle, but I think so. Yes."

"If the warbler's keeping to its regular schedule, it should leave the pines down below in about an hour."

"We didn't need to get started so early. I should have said eight-thirty, or even nine."

"You couldn't predict how long the climb would take. Besides, it's probably better to be here before the bird, instead of suddenly appearing when it's feeding or resting or whatever it does at mid-day."

"Oh. True."

With her breathing back to normal, Ivy began to notice all the noises around them. The muted tapping of a Downy Woodpecker as it dug grubs out of a rotting tree. The nasal "yank" of a nuthatch. Goldfinches overhead. Blue Jays deep in the forest. Crows crying out an alarm about a hawk or a roosting owl or maybe a hiker.

And, through and over and under it all, the sound of wind in the trees.

"Heidi noise."

"What?"

"Heidi. I must have read that book a dozen times when I was a kid. Heidi lies in the loft every night and listens to the sound of wind through the tall pines around her grandfather's hut." She chuckled. "I wanted so much to be in the Alps instead of Vermont. But really, it's probably the same sound in both places."

The man made a noise like a quiet grunt.

On the far side of the reservoir, cloud shadows chased each other up the hills, one after another, painting newly mown hayfields almost gray and then bright green. A Red-tailed Hawk alternately flapped and soared in big circles over the reservoir.

"What time is it?

"Ten-twenty."

"Getting closer."

"If the warbler's on schedule."

"True."

Ivy uncurled her legs and stretched, leaning back on stiff arms and raising her face to the sky. Beside her, Hugh made a noise low in his throat and jerked his chin toward a towering white pine.

"There. One o'clock in that tree. Something gray. I think I caught some yellow."

She scanned and then caught her breath. "Oh, good

eye. Good eye! That's it!"

The Grace's Warbler was gleaning in the top branches. They could see only gray when it had its back to them, and then white wing bars flashed as it moved, and the yellow chin and throat gleamed in the sun.

The warbler disappeared around the backside of the tree and Ivy held her breath until she saw it again, this time a little closer.

"What's it eating?"

"I don't... Oh! I just saw it. Something green. Wiggly."

"And another one."

The little bird methodically worked one long branch.

"I wish I had a good camera. Black bill, yellow forehead, yellow breast, snow white belly, bright green worm."

"The money shot."

"Ick."

"Sorry. I shouldn't have let Josef intrude." Ivy folded her legs again. "I'm glad he didn't come along today."

"Me too."

The warbler was hopping from twig to twig, checking each branch top and bottom for food. It constantly turned its head from side to side, rapidly looking to the left and the right, twisting to get a look at the underside of branches. As it came closer, they could easily follow it with their bare eyes. In slow motion, they laid their binoculars on the rock.

Suddenly the warbler stopped feeding and tilted its head back. A quick, sweet, rising chee-chee-chee-chee-chee-chee-chee rang out against the background noises of the forest. The two humans sat frozen, breathless, silent.

The bird sang again and then left the treetops and flew straight toward them, coming down beside one of the small puddles on the rocky ledge. Ivy and Hugh barely turned their heads, watching from the corners of their eyes as the little bird dipped its bill and drank and then stepped into the puddle. They could hear small splashing noises. Droplets of water glittered in the air and on the rock.

The bird finished its bath and stood beside the puddle, sunlight making a tiny rainbow on one wet wing.

Ivy cautiously turned her head farther. She realized she was holding her breath and made herself inhale slowly so she wouldn't gasp and startle the warbler.

The bird flew to a branch only a few yards away and began preening, oblivious to the watching humans, shaking its body and then its head, lifting first one wing and then the other, turning to groom the feathers with its bill.

Ivy had no idea how much time passed. She realized she was getting hot on the exposed granite shelf but there was no way that she was going to move.

The warbler flew several yards away and resumed gleaning for insects.

Ivy unfolded her legs and wiggled around until she was stretched out on her belly on the warm rock. "No one else has mentioned hearing the warbler sing."

"No." Hugh shifted a little on the hard rock. "I wonder if it always sings up here. We wouldn't hear it down on the logging trail."

"Maybe it sang down near the reservoir when it first got here. Before Charlie and Sean discovered it."

"Maybe."

"I wonder if it will eventually stop singing because it never gets an answer."

"Maybe."

The warbler was feeding less energetically now, stopping often to look around, its black eyes bright and alert.

"Maybe it just sings a little now and then. Just sending the noise out into the universe."

"Hoping it will be answered?"

"Like sending out a radio signal to find extraterrestrials."

Gradually, the warbler moved farther and farther away until it was again a little gray dot against blue-green foliage. And then they couldn't see it anymore.

Several minutes passed.

"I think the show might be over."

"Until tomorrow."

"Right."

Ivy rolled onto her back and put one arm over her face. "This was such a good idea, Hugh. I feel like we've spent hours in that little bird's world, sharing its life."

The man lying next to her was quiet so long that she wondered if he'd fallen asleep. Then—"I lied."

Ivy didn't move her arm from across her eyes. "Oh, yeah? About what?"

"When I said I no longer care about sex."

She had no idea how to answer, so she said nothing.

"Well, it was true when I told you. So I guess I didn't lie."

"I'm glad that's cleared up."

"But now I am."

"Now you are what?"

"Interested in sex."

Ivy rolled to her side and propped her head on her hand. "And you're telling me, why?"

"Because I haven't been the slightest bit interested in sex for years. Eight years. Until right now. With you." There was a bright spot of red on each of his cheekbones.

"I doubt it has anything to do with me, Hugh. We don't really know each other. We're not even sure we like each other."

Hugh raised an eyebrow.

"Okay, today has been nice. But most times I'm not sure about you, and you act like you don't always like me. At best, we might consider ourselves birding buddies. Like Jack and Charlie and me."

Again there was quiet. Ivy frowned at the ledge and the pools and the wildflowers. He had ruined the peaceful quiet of the day. She didn't want to leave but she knew she'd have to sit up soon and gather up her pack and get things back to normal.

His warm fingers touched hers. He brought her hand to the front of his trousers.

"Does Jack or Charlie get a hard-on with their 'birding buddy'?"

Ivy tried to pull away but he tightened his hold.

"We'll get up and leave in just a minute. But I want you to know what being with you right now is doing to me. Doing for me. I haven't had a real erection, except the first-thing-in-the-morning-have-to-pee kind, since the fire. Eight years now." His eyes were closed, his body taut, his jaw jutting up. "I feel like a living human right now. A man. I believed I would never feel like this again."

There was a long moment of silence. Ivy felt him

swell under her hand, get harder. She stopped trying to lift her hand.

When Hugh spoke again, his voice was thick and strained. "I don't know anything about your life. You could have a boyfriend now for all I know. But Jack said something that made me think you might be a, that you've always been alone. Is that right?"

For a split second, Ivy considered making her voice indignant, considered reminding him how very unlikely it was that a woman her age could be a virgin.

"Yes."

"So you've never felt this before? An erection? Or seen one?"

"No." Ivy curved her fingers around him. "I... No."

He pushed up against their hands. "This is unbelievably good. Literally. Unbelievable."

She didn't lift her hand when he loosened his grip. She very much wished she could see what she was touching. She didn't want to pass up this chance. She didn't want to turn thirty-six, forty, fifty, to live the rest of her life without ever having touched a man.

He was lying completely still, holding his breath, staring at the sky. "Would you... Ivy, would you be willing to touch me without my clothes in the way?"

She wondered if he'd really asked that. Maybe she'd imagined it.

She sat up, and he turned his face away, both of his hands in fists at his sides.

"Ivy, I'm sorry. We should go—"

"I couldn't open your pants from that angle." It took both of her hands to undo the button. She found the zipper pull and pulled his fly down slowly, so afraid of hurting him that she could hardly breathe.

"God."

His fingers brushed against hers as he freed himself.

Ivy stared down. She wished that he would push his pants out of the way or take them off, wished that she could see his bare legs and his belly and his chest. Wished she could see all of him.

"You can touch me any way you want." Hugh's voice was hoarse. "Or not touch me. Whatever you're all right with."

She moved just the tips of her fingers around the end and then, barely touching, down his length. He muttered something she couldn't quite hear.

"Does that… Does that feel all right?"

His breath came out in a little laugh. "I said it a minute ago. God, Ivy. Holy, mysterious, glorious, wonderful god."

Ivy cupped her other hand around him, barely touching. "This is beautiful when it's hard. I had no idea."

There was no bird song anymore, no background forest noises, no breeze, no hot sun. Ivy was breathless in quiet, intent on what she was seeing and feeling.

"It's amazing that it's so hard but your skin is so, is so incredibly soft. To touch. Silky. Warm silky."

There was a drop of moisture, and she touched it with her thumb.

"Ivy." His voice was barely recognizable.

She whispered, "What?"

"I'm not going to last very long."

"You mean you want me to stop?"

"God, no." His fingers closed around her hand and he raised it to his mouth and she watched him put his lips against her palm. "But I haven't had an orgasm in years.

Years. I'm perilously close to one and I don't want to scare you."

Ivy freed her hand from his. "I don't think I'll be scared."

He put both his hands around hers. There was nothing in her world but the smooth hardness between her hands and the sound of harsh breathing.

Then he strained upwards, a low growling moan starting in his chest and growing louder, harsher, and she felt wet warmth spurting through her fingers.

****

Ivy didn't know how long she sat, staring down, beginning to feel awkward, beginning to wonder what she was supposed to do next.

"Well, that was ridiculous." His voice was rough, almost a whisper.

She tried to pull her hands away but he held them tighter.

"I should have had my handkerchief handy. We wouldn't have ended up with cum all over our hands. I'm a bit embarrassed about that."

She raised her eyes. He was looking up at her with his face softened and relaxed, his wide mouth curving into the first real smile she'd seen. The sun washed some of the color from his dark eyes and made them look like wine.

"But at the same time, Ivy Pritchard, I am convinced that was the most perfect orgasm any man has had since Adam discovered sex."

He pulled one of his hands away, sat up and got a bandanna out of his hip pocket. "Here." He pressed the cloth against her palms, spread her fingers, dried between them while she sat mutely and watched the colors: her pale fingers, his darker ones, the purple bandanna. "You always have hand cleaner in your vest. Right?"

Ivy blinked. "Oh. Yes. Just a minute."

It was good to look away from him, to unzip the side pocket of her birding vest and take out the little bottle of hand cleaner and hand it to him. It felt ceremonial, Hugh squirting a small bit of the cleaner into one of her palms and then one of his, both of them silently rubbing their hands together, the sharp smell of alcohol in the air. Ivy made a noise that was almost a giggle and tried to cover it by turning away and putting the bottle of cleaner back in her vest pocket.

From the corner of her eye she could see him standing up. The sound when he pulled up his zipper was shockingly loud.

"Did you get wet?"

Her eyes flew to his face. "What?"

"We just had sex, you and I. Even though I was the only one who came, we both were involved. I was watching your face at the beginning. I know you were involved." The corner of his mouth twitched up. "You weren't just going through the motions. So to speak."

Ivy flushed and scrambled awkwardly to her feet.

"So did you get wet while you were touching me? Between your legs?"

She bent and picked up her hat.

"Were you disgusted by what just happened?"

"No. Let's go."

"Were you embarrassed?"

"I'm not disgusted. I'm not embarrassed. Let's head back to the car."

"So you weren't embarrassed by what my body does

when I'm turned on, when I'm having sex, when I experience orgasm. But you're embarrassed by how your body feels when you're turned on?"

"For Pete's sake, Hugh." She turned away from him and looked around on the ground, checking for anything they might have left behind, just like she always did after any stop on a birding walk. "I'm a thirty-five-year old virgin. *Everyone*'s embarrassed when someone like me feels, feels turned on."

"I'm not. Not the slightest bit."

She frowned at him, her cheeks red and her eyes stormy. "Yes. I got wet."

"Are you still wet?"

"Yes. I'm still wet."

"Would you let me touch you there?"

"No."

"Do you understand that I would be gratified if you'd let me reciprocate?"

"I… No."

Hugh stared at her and she stared back, willing him to look away and change the subject and let her go. After a long moment, his face hardened.

"I see. We'd better head back. It's clouding over. It's a long hike to the car."

They walked in silence through the darkening woods. Once Ivy heard a Wood Thrush close by and she knew Hugh wanted to get a better look at one but she didn't say anything. She wanted to be back in her car, back in her room behind the shop. She wanted to be alone. She wanted to relive touching Hugh's penis, the first she'd ever touched.

****

"Ivy. Stop." They were close to the parking lot,

hearing cars going by on the road. She kept walking until he reached out and grabbed her elbow. "Stop. Ivy. Stop. You're still upset."

She whirled, suddenly so angry that she thought her head might explode. "Upset? Of course I'm upset! I feel stupid. And abnormal…" Her voice broke. "And…And stupid."

He studied her face. "Ivy, you gave me an extraordinary gift today. The last thing in the world I want is for you to feel sad. It's… it's all right."

"No it is not all right! It's not. Any normal woman would have wanted you to, to help her come. Any *normal* woman wouldn't still be a virgin after today! If I were a normal woman, I would have heard… heard…"

Her eyes filled with tears.

"Heard what?"

She glared at him. "That noise you made. I should have heard it while you were on top of me. While you were inside me. Not when I was sitting beside you on a hard rock. It's *not* all right, to be not normal. I hate it!"

They stood in quiet, Ivy holding her chin up belligerently, Hugh watching her with his dark eyes puzzled and unhappy. Then she slumped. "I'm sorry. I don't want to take away any of the happiness you showed up there."

"Nothing could take away that happiness, Ivy." He reached out his hand but dropped it without touching her. "But tell me you enjoyed it a little. Me a huge amount, but you a little too. Please."

"You are an absurdly persistent person. Okay. I liked touching you and I've never done that before."

His teeth flashed briefly in the gathering gloom. Even in the growing darkness, she could see his face soften and his mouth relax.

"Good. I'm glad. Thank you."

"So, we're both happy. Let's go."

He watched in silence as she turned away and started walking.

"Where did Charlie put my keys?"

"Big maple, I think he said. Barbed wire... Yes, right here."

As she put the keys into his palm, Hugh closed his hand and his long fingers slid along hers. "I thank you again for a memorable afternoon of birding and other natural happenings."

"You're welcome." She pulled her hand away.

Hugh slid behind the wheel and started the engine. "Seat belt."

"Oh. Yes."

"It's a good thing I've been through here a few times before. This could be tricky without good light."

"Yes."

Ivy shifted so she could watch his face. "Are you religious?"

"What?"

"You kept saying god."

He glanced over at her, his quick smile lifting the corner of his mouth. "Oh. That. No. I'm not religious. I just invoke the deity at moments of emotion." His voice broke. "And ecstasy."

"Oh."

"What about you? What are your sounds at moments of ecstasy?"

"I'm uncomfortable with this. I shouldn't have started on this subject."

"All right."

They didn't talk again until Hugh stopped next to Ivy's Fiat in the Montpelier park-and-ride.

"I want one more thing."

She turned toward him, her eyes wary.

"I want to know that you're going to take care of the tension I caused for you today. I want you to go home and give yourself a wonderful orgasm, safe in your own bed."

She stared at him. Then she shook her head hard and opened the door.

He sat watching as she got into her Fiat, as she drove halfway across the lot, as she stopped her car and backed up, as she lowered her window and leaned her head out.

"Hugh? Thank you for the warbler."

Chapter Thirteen

Hot humid days brought thunderstorms, every afternoon and into every night. The forest around the reservoir was pummeled by wind and driving rain. The robin lost the three eggs from her second clutch when strong winds whipped the tree branch back and forth and sent the nest flying off into the night. Four young flickers drowned after a big old oak uprooted and went crashing to the forest floor, landing with the nesting cavity open to the downpour.

The little Wood-Pewee rode out the storms in her lichen-covered nest firmly attached to a sturdy branch. She flattened her body to protect her young from the rain and waited for each new day when her mate would again bring food to her.

The Grace's Warbler had no mate to feed, no nestlings to protect. Every afternoon, as the thunder grew louder and lightning bathed the forest in flashes of white light, the bird retreated to its night roost close to the trunk of a sturdy pine.

Chapter Fourteen

Ivy groaned and tossed her pillow as far as she could across the small space in the back of her shop.

Another night of sleep ruined. It was too late to try to go back to sleep. She had to get ready for today's FATSO walk.

He wouldn't show up. She hoped. Surely. He wouldn't. He wouldn't show up.

****

"Too bad that man never smiles 'cause that is one fine bod."

Ivy froze in the act of getting her tripod out of the back seat of the car.

Beside her, Molly made a small purring noise. "And those jeans do great things for his legs and butt! Way better than those baggy pants with all those pockets."

Ivy had a startlingly vivid recollection of her hands undoing those baggy pants. She could feel the round metal button, the zipper, see her fingers trembling, feel the hot sun on her back.

She straightened, giving her whole body a little shake. She could do this. If he wasn't going to be embarrassed, she wouldn't be either. This was just a bird walk, a regular bird walk.

She followed Molly's gaze to the group a few yards away. Jack was talking in his usual animated fashion, with his voice and his hands, his eyes sparkling. Charlie was grinning and even Josef had a slight smile on his face. Only Hugh looked somber. He was standing slightly apart from the others, rolling up his shirtsleeves. Early morning sun flickering through the trees turned the hair on his arms from brown to red.

No one would ever guess what parts of Hugh's body she'd seen. His bare feet. His ankles. His scar.

His penis. And now, for the first time, his arms.

She realized with a start that Hugh had raised his eyes and was watching her, his eyes dark and intent.

"Okay!" She said loudly. "We have a challenge today! We *have* to find a Marsh Wren for our Mr. Carmichael."

****

The wetlands were alive with Red-winged Blackbirds, the glossy males singing from the tops of cattails and the brown striped females lurking near the ground where the nests were. Goldfinches flew over the birders, sounding their little "potato chip" noise at the bottom of every swoop. A cardinal, hidden in a tangle of sumac and grapevines, filled the air with loud sweet whistles. Along the hedge-rows, Song Sparrows and Savannah Sparrows tilted back their heads and sang.

And from the marshes came rattling, chirping, scolding noises.

"Wrens," Jack muttered. "I hear 'em. But I can't see 'em."

"They come to the top of the cattails pretty often," Ivy whispered, "but just a second at a time. You've just got to be looking in the right direction at the right moment."

"Over there." Molly nudged Jack's arm without lowering her binoculars.

"Oh, good eye, Molly! Yes! Got it, Jack?"

"I... No... YES!" He winced and lowered his voice. "Yes! I see it!"

"And we're going to get a good long look! See what it's doing?"

The tiny brown bird was tucking a long piece of grass into a tennis-ball-sized clump hanging between two cattails.

"Is that a nest? I'm gonna get to see the bird *and* its nest??"

"It's definitely a nest. The entrance must be around the back." Ivy slowly moved her scope into position.

"This is awesome. My life as a birder is complete." Jack bent over the scope. "I was beginning to think that the words on my gravestone would be *He Never Got a Marsh Wren*."

****

Ivy watched the others out of the corner of her eye. Hugh was standing between Beck and Josef, his head tilted a little as he listened to something Beck was saying. Ivy felt illogically abandoned, illogically ticked off. He hadn't once acknowledged her presence. He hadn't once met her eyes. He hadn't once treated her like a woman who had given him—in his own words—the most perfect orgasm in history.

She hadn't expected him to call. Of course not. Or drop by the shop. She didn't know what people usually did after having had sex on a ledge. But she had expected *something*, some sign that something had happened between the two of them.

****

Molly pulled into the park-and-ride and waved at Charlie, Josef, and Beck, all in their own cars and ready to head home.

Across the lot, Jack bent to say something through the window of Hugh's car then headed toward his own little vehicle, getting out his cellphone as he walked.

"Betcha five bucks he's calling Rose."

Ivy snorted. "Only a sucker would take that bet, Moll. He calls his wife as soon as he gets back after every outing." Even at a distance, they could see Jack's face crease with a broad smile, his eyes crinkle up, his cheeks get rounder. "Even before she was pregnant."

"Get a load of our Mr. MacDougal."

Ivy looked over at the Audi station wagon. Hugh's binoculars were up to his face and he was focused on the grassy area between the parking lot and the road.

"The man is hooked, Ivy. When a new birder starts looking for birds when he's not actually birding, he's well and truly hooked. I can't imagine there'd be much right there, though."

"Sparrows?"

Molly picked up her own binoculars and focused on the grassy area. "I can't see anything. There might be lots of seeds on the ground, though." She lowered her binoculars. "Maybe that'll be his specialty. Hugh's. Like some guys become experts on gulls and all their different plumages."

"And it's always guys. With gulls. For some reason."

"True. That's weird. Anyway, Hugh can be the BBC expert on sparrows." Molly lifted her binoculars again. "We could go ask him what he saw."

"Nah. Your grandkids expect you. You don't want to start discussing a mystery this late."

Molly sighed. "Birding is done for the day. Why is

104

that always so hard to accept?"

Ivy bent and picked up her water bottle and field notebook from the floor of the car.

"Look at Jack. Still on the phone. He's going to see his Rose in a few minutes but they have so much to talk about anyway."

Jack was leaning against his car, laughing, his short legs crossed at the ankles. The turquoise-colored Smart Car with the brown scales and the fishy eyeballs looked like a gaudy toy in front of two green dumpsters side-by-side at the back edge of the lot.

"I wonder if Jack will get a bigger car once the baby's born."

"He'll have to. Otherwise he'll have to decide between a baby seat and his wife every time he goes any... Whoa! That's weird!"

Behind Jack, one of the huge dumpsters was slowly lifting into the air.

"Oh! There's a garbage truck on the other side. That looked totally mysterious for a second there."

"Dumpster levitation." Ivy bent to get her scope out of the back seat. She whirled around when Molly suddenly leaned on the horn and yelled Jack's name.

The dumpster was now above the height of Jack's car, and it was tipping forward.

The two women saw Jack look up and wave. They saw him notice the dark shape out of the corner of his eye. They saw him take two steps forward before the heavy dumpster wavered and fell, crushing the little car and knocking him to the ground.

"Call 9-1-1." Molly was out of her car and already running. She yelled back over her shoulder, "First-aid kit in the trunk. Bring it!"

Molly and Hugh got to him at the same time, Molly touching her fingers to Jack's throat and Hugh pushing apart the edges of a long bloody rip in the fallen man's pant leg.

"Pulse okay but he's out." Molly ran practiced hands over Jack's neck, shoulders, and ribs. "Ivy. Open the kit and hand me a couple of the big gauze pads. And give some to Hugh."

Jack moaned and tried to get his arms under his chest to push himself up, but Molly and Hugh each put a hand on his back.

"You're all right, Jack." Molly's often raucous voice was gentle and even. "Don't move. Give us a few minutes to see what's what." She gently cleared blood from his face and then pressed the pad to a gash above one ear. "Hugh, how's the leg?'

"Wide scrape. Long." Two of the thick pads were already wet through and Hugh dropped them to the pavement and reached up for more.

Molly gently probed the back of Jack's neck and down his spine. "Jack? Can you open your eyes for me?"

"Was that a *dumpster* that hit me?" His clear, loud voice startled all three of them.

"It was indeed. Can you open your eyes?"

"Sure. But all I see is pavement."

"Sorry I can't get you a better view but we don't want to move you until the ambulance gets here."

"And red. I see blood." His breath was coming in short bursts.

"You've got a cut on your scalp. Anything on the head bleeds like crazy." She held out a hand and Ivy handed her another gauze pad. "Is this just water in your bottle, Jack?"

"Water. Yes."

Molly handed the bottle up to Ivy and waited, her hand out, while Ivy soaked the pad with water. "This will help." She held the pad over Jack's eye and wiped blood up and away.

Jack blinked. "Better." He turned his head a little in one direction and then the other. "Head stings. Leg hurts. I'm sitting up. Don't stop me."

Hugh jerked and held out both hands but Molly made a little gesture and he backed off. They watched as Jack got to his hands and knees and then awkwardly rolled to a sitting position with his legs straight out in front of him.

Ivy could hear a siren in the distance.

"Lucky the whole thing didn't hit me." Jack reached out and touched two metal handles jutting out from the shiny green dumpster. "Just these doodads I think." He stared at his fingers. "Yup. Blood."

"Any pain in your belly?"

"Told you. Head and leg."

Hugh had both hands on Jack's calf again, pressing hard, holding the edges of the long gash together. There was a growing pool of blood on the black pavement, red and shiny in the sun.

Jack surprised them a second time, this time by laughing. "You two. Molly. Hugh. Mismatched pair of angels."

****

"So what's the word?" Ivy stood up as Molly came back into the waiting room.

"Forty-two stitches on his calf and sixteen on his head. A few pints of blood. IV drip, antibiotics. Possible concussion. They're going to keep him overnight."

"You saved his life, Molly."

"Hugh and I just did basic first aid."

"I meant yelling and blowing the horn."

"Oh. Yes. I forgot."

"You look really shaken up, Moll."

"I am. Look at me." She held out her hands. "I handled blood and bodies every single day for over twenty years, but today really got to me. I kept thinking about Rose, and the baby, and…" Her voice broke. "And how happy Jack always is."

Ivy had never once known Molly to lose her cheerful flippancy. She felt her own eyes stinging as she put her arms around the older woman.

"Jack is your friend. That makes it different."

After just a few moments, Molly stood back. She straightened her back, lifted her chin, blinked several times, and took a deep breath. "Okay. I'm fine now."

"When will he be able to go home?"

"Probably tomorrow afternoon." Molly's little face was puzzled and frowning, her blue eyes still swimming with tears. "I had a crust, Ivy. A hard crust. When I was working. Nothing got through. I could shove some guy's guts back in and then go home and make supper with Ed, and laugh and talk and be normal." She looked away. "It's been only two years but I've lost the crust."

"Come on. I'll drive you home."

"One thing's for sure. Whether or not Jack keeps that little car is no longer in question."

****

Ivy didn't look up when she heard Molly enter the store. "Twenty-eight binocs, Moll!" She crowed. "That teacher came back and bought the four we had *and* ordered two dozen more! Turns out the whole school is into bird-watching!" Ivy slammed the cash register drawer triumphantly. "The biggest order ever."

Her wide grin faded when she turned and saw Molly's face.

"Jack's back in the hospital, Ivy. In the ICU. Infection." Her little face was taut, her hands clenched into tight fists. "Where I worked before, three people died in one infectious outbreak. Superbugs. They don't respond to most antibiotics." She shuddered. "Took one guy two weeks to die. The staff tried everything, one thing after another, but it wasn't any more scientific than throwing darts and praying."

"Sit. Sit." Ivy wheeled her desk chair out from the back room. "How'd Jack get the infection? From the pavement?"

"Best guess? He got it in the hospital. Most people who get sick from antibiotic-resistant bacteria pick 'em up in a hospital."

"That's scary. Go into the hospital to be taken care of and get a deadly infection."

"Scary for the hospital staff too." She swallowed and looked away.

For the second time in a week, Ivy put her arms around her friend.

"I gotta tell you, Ivy." Molly swallowed a sob. "I'm scared."

"We can't see him, right?"

"Definitely not. He's going to be quarantined till the infection's gone." She moved back a little and dug a tissue out of her pocket. "We've got to do something. The FATSO group. Yes. I know." She straightened her shoulders. "Food. Rose will be at the hospital most of the time. We'll go fill the fridge with ready-to-eat stuff and put casseroles or something in the freezer."

"Great idea, Moll. I'll send around an e-mail."

****

"I hope that's not salads, Charlie." Molly was in front of the open refrigerator. "We've got salads up the whazzoo."

"Nope." Charlie and Hugh put two grocery bags on the counter in Rose's kitchen and started unloading milk, orange juice, yogurt, and cottage cheese. "Small containers. Wasteful. But we figured Rose is gonna be opening things and then forgetting about them."

Hugh finished emptying his bag onto the counter. "If we could have found a half-dozen donuts and half a loaf of bread, we would've grabbed them."

Beck lifted a canvas bag onto the butcherblock island. "Is there room in the freezer for two casserole dishes, Molly?"

Josef peered into the bag. "Two dishes, Beck. What's in 'em?"

She took a foil-wrapped dish out of the canvas bag. "Chicken cacciatore. For later."

"Visiting hours? The wake?" He looked up when Molly inhaled sharply. "What?! I'm being realistic. Lots of people don't beat those superbugs. That's why they call 'em super."

Two bright spots of color appeared on Beck's cheekbones. "This is for when Jack is *home*."

"Where'd you get the chicken?"

"What?"

"You heard me."

The others stiffened at his tone.

"It's one of the Buff Orpingtons."

"Uh uh. Not acceptable, Beck. Not acceptable at all.

Those hens were still laying. I got them for eggs."

"A few of them are laying hens. The others were bred for meat." Beck's whole body was rigid. "Jack is a friend. You were gone. You had my car. I couldn't go to the store. I killed one of the chickens." She turned. "Watch your head, Molly."

The kitchen was silent as Beck opened the freezer, put the two dishes inside and then stood motionless, her back to the rest of the room.

"Chicken cacciatore is Jack's favorite."

"Touching." Josef was no longer smiling. "You and Jack got something going, Beck? He been cheating on his pregnant wife?"

She wheeled, picked up her canvas bag, and stalked out of the room. She didn't slow down, or even seem to notice, when she almost collided with Ivy at the door.

Ivy looked around the silent kitchen. Josef's back was to her, his shoulders tight and his fists clenching and unclenching. Molly was standing near the refrigerator, pale and tense. Across the room, Hugh and Charlie were staring at Josef, their eyes cold.

"What's… Is Beck okay?"

Josef turned, smiling again. "Moody. Must be that time of the month."

Charlie dug into the bottom of his shopping bag and pulled out four large bars of dark chocolate. "My grandson tells me it chases away demonizers or some such thing." He broke one of the bars into pieces. "Molly. Hugh. Eat it."

"Don't mind if I do." Josef reached out and took one of the biggest chunks. "What you got there, Ivy?"

She met Molly's eyes, puzzled. When the older woman gave a little headshake, Ivy set down a large

111

rectangular pan, a roll of foil and a box of freezer bags. "This is huge but I'm going to divide it up."

Josef sniffed. "Smells great. Lasagna. You got some Italian in you?" He stared into her face. "The dark hair fits. But not that skin. All those Mediterranean types are dark. Swarthy."

Ivy lifted out a square of lasagna and placed it on a piece of tinfoil. "It's from Guido's. I don't cook."

"You're puttin' us on. What do you eat?"

She shrugged. "Mexican take-out from Jorge's, Italian take-out from Guido's, salads from the co-op or the IGA." She tucked the foil around the piece of lasagna and set it aside. "For one person alone, it works great."

Molly made an odd little movement, as if shaking herself all over, and embraced the new topic with visible relief. "But you used to cook, didn't you?"

"I cooked for my folks for a few months, after my mother had a stroke. It was pretty boring. They wouldn't try anything new." Still puzzled, she looked over at the two silent men by the counter. "So I did the tuna mac, and the mashed potatoes and meatloaf and frozen peas, and the wieners and beans." She finished wrapping a second piece of lasagna, set it aside, and lifted out another square. "And the occasional spaghetti with Ragu when my father felt like being cosmopolitan." She set aside the third wrapped serving. "And before that, at the commune, I ate in the community dining hall."

"Commune, huh? You lived in a commune?" Josef waggled his eyebrows. "Free love and all that?"

Ivy glanced up and met Hugh's dark eyes for just an instant before she looked back down at the almost-empty pan. The only person who knew she hadn't had wild sex when she was in her twenties, when she was living in a commune, the only person who knew she was still a virgin, was the newcomer.

"Woooo. Look at that blush!" Josef's rich baritone filled the room. "Come on, Ivy, spill! One special guy? Lots of guys? Gals? Guys and gals together? Orgies?"

From the corner of her eye, Ivy saw Hugh take two steps closer.

But it was Charlie who spoke. "Going for a full sweep, Josef? Everyone disgusted with you at the same time?"

"What the hell? I'm just trying to lighten the mood!" Josef looked around. "Jeez. Sourpusses. I'm outa here."

They all watched him leave, and they all heard him slam the door.

Ivy looked around at the others. "What on earth happened in here?"

"Nothing we haven't seen before, Ivy. Just more obnoxious than usual." Molly turned to Hugh, her face speculative. "And you. You looked like you were getting ready to do some physical damage."

He was still glaring at the doorway, his body stiff. "I asked this before. I'm going to ask it again. Is Beck in physical danger?"

"We've thought about that. We think Josef is verbally abusive, but that's all."

"So far." Hugh folded the grocery bags with jerky motions. "You ready, Charlie?"

"Yeah." He looked around. "Eat the chocolate."

As they walked out the door, Charlie looked like he could be Hugh's older brother, his legs almost as long, his shoulders as wide, his back as straight.

"Well. That's cute." Molly put the lid on a giant cooler and snapped it shut. "It looks like our two men of few words might have a friendship going."

Ivy blinked. "They came together?"

"Yes. And I think they went grocery shopping together."

Ivy started to smile. "I can see it. Striding through the IGA. Each with his own basket."

"Speaking in monosyllables."

"Pulling out their wallets simultaneously."

"Splitting the cost. Without discussing it."

Ivy nodded. "Cute."

Chapter Fifteen

A rushing sound above and behind gave the Grace's Warbler a split second's warning. It lurched sideways and up, into the woods, centimeters ahead of razor-tipped talons. The warbler and the Sharp-shinned Hawk rocketed through the forest, the one intent on escape and the other intent on eating. The little warbler would be the hawk's first meal in many hours. It was not about to let it go. But then the smaller bird turned sharply around an ancient hickory. Before it could correct its headlong rush, the hawk barreled past. Tiny heart pounding, the warbler took shelter way in on a branch, against the shaggy tree trunk. Almost an hour passed before it risked moving again.

And now, for two days, the warbler had been aware of human activity on the broad ledge. It was aware of muted conversation and backpacks and canvas blinds and plastic boxes full of equipment. It was aware of the two mist nets with thousands of sparkling dewdrops catching the morning sun. But days of heavy rain had left the treetops full of water, with tiny pools wherever horizontal branches flattened out or dipped, so the bird didn't have to come down to the ledge to drink or bathe. It stayed away from the quiet intent humans and all their equipment and went about its daily routine. It gleaned for insects in the tall white pines at the northern end of the reservoir, rested in the trees near the ledge in the afternoon, and then fed again near the logging trail before spending the night tucked in against the trunk of a towering white pine.

The next morning, the humans were visible, as they had been for days, but they were far away, crouched down beside the trail that led through the meadow. The warbler spent a few minutes preening on a branch near the ledge. Nothing alerted it to danger. Nothing was moving below. With heavy cloud cover, no sun illuminated the drops of dew in the mist nets.

The bird fluttered down to drink and bathe in a tiny pool. When it lifted off, it flew directly into a net. Once, when the bird had flown into a spider's web, it had freed itself with just a brief struggle. But struggling now entangled it more and more. After a while, the bird stopped moving. It hung almost upside down, wrapped in the thin mesh.

Chapter Sixteen

"Charlie? Is that your name? Charlie, you stand over here. Fasten this onto your collar."

The television film crew had split into two. One camera and one interviewer were in Ivy's shop early in the morning, before the mall opened, and the other camera and the rest of the crew were with the field scientists on the ledge overlooking the reservoir.

"Your little warbler is big news. We had a reporter out there yesterday who talked with people from seven states and three Canadian provinces."

"Must be a slow news week."

The woman laughed. "Well, yes. But this'll interest people." She looked around and pointed to Molly. "You. You're short. Why don't you perch on this stool? Ivy, you should be behind the counter. Where's the boy who saw the warbler first? Is he coming?"

Charlie finished fastening the tiny microphone to his shirt and looked up. "Be here in a minute. Name's Sean."

"Good. Always a better story with kids. Now, you all know we might not use the interviews we're going to do today, right?" She handed mics to Molly and Ivy. "If they don't get the warbler today, we're taking off for Maine. There's a White-faced Ibis at Scarborough Marsh. I gather it's supposed to be out west, like your warbler. Fasten it like this." She helped Molly attach the tiny mic to her sweater. "If they get the warbler, great.

But if they don't, we'll fill the slot with the ibis."

She had a few words with the cameraman and then asked, "So what's going on up on the hill?"

"They'll be checking the mist nets soon. If the warbler gets anywhere near that ledge, they should get it."

There was a knock on the door to the back parking lot and Charlie went to let Sean in.

"Good." The interviewer laid a small notebook on the counter. "The guy from the Cornell Lab will be here soon but we can get started without him. Sean, you're the star. Just tell the story. And relax."

Sean looked over at his grandfather, who gave him a thumbs-up. "I'm ready."

She pointed to the silent man with the video camera. "That's Eddie. Don't look at Eddie while we're recording. Look at me. I'm Ann."

She turned toward the camera and smiled. Her shoulders were back, her hair freshly brushed, her lipstick refreshed, her expression calm, and her voice smooth and professional.

"On yesterday's evening news, we talked with two men who traveled all the way from northern Maine, just to see a tiny scrap of a bird that weighs less than half an ounce. This amazing little bird is a Grace's Warbler, a species that is usually found in just a few places in the southwestern United States. Today, scientists from the Vermont Center for Ecostudies, or VCE, are up in the hills not far from Montpelier, where the warbler has been seen by excited bird-watchers from almost two dozen states and at least three Canadian provinces. They plan to catch the Grace's Warbler in a net, then weigh it, get some photographs, and snip a tiny bit of feather. That bit of feather will be analyzed in the lab, and the scientists will be able to discover exactly where the bird started its long journey and where it stopped to feed along the way.

"But they also want to know where the bird will go once it leaves Vermont. So they will be giving the warbler a little backpack, a geolocator." She pronounced the word carefully. "The geolocator will sit like a tiny backpack between the warbler's wings. Wherever the bird goes, the geolocator will record light levels, and that will help scientists determine where the bird has been." She smiled into the camera. "Of course, the scientists will have to get the geolocator back before they can analyze it. They hope that the bird will be netted again sometime and that whoever nets it will contact VCE using the e-mail or phone information included in the backpack."

She turned to Sean. "You were the first Vermonter to see this very special bird. In fact, you're the very first person to ever see a Grace's Warbler in the whole northeast. Tell us what you thought when you first saw it."

****

No one appeared to be in any hurry to leave. Sean was perched on the stool that was usually behind the counter, flushed from the success of his interview. Charlie and Hugh stood next to the chain gate, listening attentively to the Cornell ornithology professor who had just finished explaining on camera why birds sometimes become vagrants. Eddie with the camera and Ann the interviewer were huddled against the wall, reviewing video footage and talking in low tones.

Ivy raised her voice. "Okay, everyone. We've got a half hour before the store opens. Let's get the display cases and bookshelves back where they belong. Then you're all welcome to wait here for the call from the ledge."

"Did you move everything yourself this morning?" Hugh's deep voice was suddenly at her shoulder.

"Molly helped."

"You should have asked everyone to come early and set things up."

"I needed time to figure out where we were going to put everything. Sometimes lots of eager volunteers is chaos rather than help."

She jumped off the counter and put both hands on the side of a wooden bookcase.

"For god's sake, Ivy. That's heavy. I'm right here. Let me do it." He slid the case back into place with little apparent effort. "This one goes here, right?"

Ivy nodded, and Hugh pulled another loaded bookcase back into its usual place.

The man from Cornell slapped his hand to his hip pocket and pulled out his phone. "Here it is. The call. Keep your fingers crossed."

There was silence. Then—"They got the warbler. Success! They're fitting him right now with the backpack."

The small shop rang with cheers and congratulations.

"So we'll be on TV now, right? They'll use our interviews?"

Charlie reached out and ruffled his grandson's hair. "Yours, definitely. You and that warbler are the stars!"

****

"Do you have a few minutes? I'd like to talk with you." Hugh was again at her elbow, looking somber and determined.

"I open that gate in about two minutes, Hugh. So no."

He looked into her face for a long minute and then wheeled and walked away.

****

"You know, Molly? I'm pooped. I'm actually hoping we get absolutely no customers at all, all day. Then you and I can take turns napping in the back room."

"I'm sort of wired. That was fun, Ivy. I learned a lot from the Cornell guy, and Sean was awesome, and you and Hugh will both look great on TV." She grinned. "Woman to woman, I see a lot of sensual promise in that lanky body and that wide mouth. And the clipped beard speaks to me of intriguing restraint. And that voice. Women all over the state are going to start watching birds after hearing that voice on the news today." She raised both eyebrows. "I'm telling you, Ivy. If I were twenty years younger, and if I weren't utterly devoted to my Ed, I might put some real effort into getting our Hugh to put his neat beard and his firm mouth against my bare torso and say something, just so I could feel that deep voice resonating in my innards."

"Goodness, Molly!" Ivy's ducked behind the counter to hide her scarlet face. "My goodness."

Chapter Seventeen

The humans were gone, taking with them their nets and their tents and their backpacks full of equipment. The Grace's Warbler didn't return to the ledge for many days. It spent most of its time feeding in the white pines nearer the reservoir, flying up to the woods by the ledge only when the sun was low on the horizon. For part of every day, the bird preened with unusual attention and vigor. It repeatedly smoothed other feathers over the one that the humans had clipped. It twisted its head and tried to peck at the flat stiff weight on its back. But it wasn't able to touch the geolocator.

Chapter Eighteen

The birders could still hear the Warbling Vireo's incessant sweet high song as they headed back to the cars.

"That little guy is incredible. I don't think he's stopped singing since we first heard him, and that was what? Almost three hours ago."

"We're so lucky we found the nest. Or rather, we're so lucky that Sean found it."

The boy looked pleased and embarrassed. "I got some great pictures on my new phone. I think you can even see the spider webs holding the nest onto that branch." He started slapping his pockets. "Oh, no! No! My mom's gonna kill me."

"What's the matter?"

"My cell phone! I don't have my cell phone!"

"When's the last time you remember having it?"

"At the vireo nest! No! At that weird mushroom. Remember? I took a picture of that weird orange mushroom. Near that huge boulder!" He made a fist and bounced it off his forehead. "Dumb, dumb, dumb!"

Charlie frowned. "Can't go back, Sean. Your mom's expecting me to get you home for lunch."

Ivy touched Sean's hand. "Stop with the pounding. You'll give yourself brain damage. I'll go back and get it. I know just where we were. You can come by the store tomorrow and pick it up."

"Oh gosh Ivy. That would be awesome. I don't want you to have to do it but I can't, can't, can't lose that phone. Thank you, thank you, thank you. I owe you humongously."

"Next time I need muscle power to move things around in the store, I'll give you a call." She turned back toward the trail.

"It's clouding over. I'm coming with you."

Hugh hadn't said two words the whole morning. Now Ivy turned to him, frowning. "I go birding by myself all the time. Even with clouds. I don't need a protector."

He looked stubborn and determined. "I'm coming."

There was a brief awkward standoff. Then Ivy shrugged and stalked out of the lot.

****

"You're not happy about this. Are you?"

"No. I mean I'm not unhappy about it. It's fine."

"Are you worried the others will start putting us together in their minds?"

She looked at him incredulously. "Like in middle school? Hugh and Ivy sittin' in a tree?"

"What?"

"The chant. You know."

"I don't know."

"For Pete's sake. How did you grow up in this country and not know? It's a taunt." She made her voice singsong. "Blank and Blank sittin' in a tree. K-I-S-S-I-N-G."

"Is that the whole thing?"

"Then there's something about a baby carriage. The two people named are supposed to be embarrassed."

"Oh."

"How did we get on this absurd topic?"

"Because you wouldn't want anyone chanting about us. Because you were embarrassed that the others saw us heading off together, just you and me."

"Not true, Hugh. Drop it."

They walked quickly and in silence, retracing the group's steps.

"We went off the trail right about here, right?"

"I think so."

"There was an animal trail. We followed it to a little clearing. With Sean's mushroom."

Hugh looked around. "I think it's… Yes. It's up there."

The animal trail was much fainter with clouds overhead than it had been earlier in the bright sun.

"I'm not sure this is the right path."

"Me neither."

But they walked only a few more yards and then they were in the clearing with the huge flat boulder in the middle and the orange mushroom glowing in the shadows. They walked around the boulder, Hugh looking and feeling around on the uneven mossy top and Ivy looking at her feet.

"Got it!" Ivy straightened, the phone in her hand. "Let's go."

"Do you really think the others can tell?"

"Can tell what?"

"That you've had your hands on my cock."

Ivy spun around.

He was staring at her face, frowning a little. "Do you think they can tell just by looking at the two of us?"

"No!"

"Then why are you so upset?"

"I'm not at all upset. I just think it's ridiculous for you to—what?—escort me up here to get Sean's phone. Chaperone me? Guard me?"

"It's not just my joining you today. Yesterday at your shop, for the interviews, you would barely meet my eyes. This morning in the parking lot I touched your arm and you jumped away. And your eyes flicked around to make sure no one else saw."

Ivy was suddenly furious. "No need to fret, Hugh MacDougal. No need at all! No one would ever suspect that we have a secret. Because *you* don't blush or jump away. You look at me the same way you look at everyone else. Completely unemotional. Completely aloof. Cool Hugh." She turned away. Her next words came to him over her shoulder. "Looking at you, no one would ever guess, not in a million years, that I've ever touched you in any way."

Hugh made her stop again by putting his hands on her shoulders. "I am *not* aloof around you. I get breathless around you ever since that day on the ledge." He took a step forward and she felt his next words against her ear. "I was so excited that day about finally getting a hard-on? Well, it keeps happening." He pulled her back until she felt the warmth from his long body. "I headed off into the woods twice this morning, Ivy, twice on that short walk. I don't have to pee that often. I just needed to be away from you, to think about compost."

"Beg your pardon?"

She felt his chest move with a short harsh laugh.

"It's a strategy. To stop thinking about sex. I see myself digging up my compost pile. Looking down at rotting food. Worms. Buzzing flies." He pulled her still closer and rubbed his cheek against her hair, moving his hands slowly down her arms. His deep quiet voice vibrated inside her. "When I was a teenager, it was bait pails. Thinking about fish bait helped whenever I got an erection at an inopportune time. Now it's compost."

He slid one arm in front of her and very gently cupped his hand, his fingers curling between her legs, feeling her heat. "I keep thinking about you here. Wanting to touch you here."

With the tips of his fingers, he traced her soft mound.

She couldn't breathe. The abrupt change from anger to melting hunger made her dizzy. She felt herself sagging against him.

"Open your pants for me."

Her fingers fumbled with the catch on her belt. He didn't help. She could feel his breath against her hair and hear its harshness.

Finally, she opened the belt and the snap and the zipper, and he slipped his hand inside.

"Hold onto your pants with one hand so they don't come all the way down. There's poison ivy."

"Oh!" Her breath came out in a gasp. "Don't want that all over my clothes."

"No."

She felt him doing what she always did, but it was so different. So different to have his bigger, rougher finger touching her there. So different to have his warm hard chest behind her. So different to feel his breath against her hair. So different to be standing up. So different not to be alone.

She closed her eyes.

And there was nothing in the world again, the same as when she'd touched him on the ledge. There was only sensation and immense quiet.

****

"I loved feeling you come. Hearing you."

Red rushed up her neck and into her cheeks. "I don't usually make noise."

"Because you don't usually have orgasms that good?"

She took a step forward, immediately feeling the loss of his hard warmth at her back, and fastened her pants with shaking hands. "It's true then, what they say. Men always want applause."

"Am I right?"

"Yes, you're right. That was amazing." She cleared her throat. "Thank you."

"Any time." He reached out both hands and caressed her shoulders. "I mean that."

"Shit."

"I offer to give you amazing orgasms any time, on demand, and you say shit?"

"There's someone coming," she whispered.

Now they could both hear people talking, coming down the hill on the trail. Hugh took Ivy's arm and pulled her behind the boulder as a woman's voice came to them, raised in indignation or disbelief. "How can she possibly like the monkey more than her own sister?! I mean, her sister is boring as hell, but that monkey is a totally foul creature!"

Ivy's giggle sounded loud in the quiet forest and Hugh pulled her closer, her nose and mouth against the warm taut skin of his neck. She smelled soap or shaving cream, a little sweat, laundry detergent. She was aware of tingling in her breasts, a renewed throbbing ache low in her belly. They could both hear the other hikers passing them, heading down the trail, still talking.

"Let me go," she whispered. "This feels silly." She pulled away and tried to make her voice light. "Do you suppose she really likes the monkey more than her sister?"

Hugh reached forward and brushed her shoulder. "Spider."

"Oh. Thanks." She swallowed. "They don't even know us. It was silly for us to act like we had to hide."

"We wouldn't want complete strangers thinking we'd been K-I-S-S-I-N-G." He reached his hand up again, this time stroking his fingers along the side of her neck.

"Another spider?"

"No. Did you feel frightened?"

"I like spiders."

"When you came. Were you afraid when I touched you? When you came?"

Her eyes widened. "Oh. No. I wasn't. At all."

"Good."

"You sort of snuck up on me. I didn't have time to think ahead. And then…" Her voice died and she looked away. "And then I couldn't think anyway."

"Do you think you might want to touch me again sometime?"

Ivy backed up several steps. "No. Yes."

"Would you come home with me right now?"

"No."

"Well." He straightened his shoulders. "That will have to do me. Knowing that you weren't afraid of me. Knowing that you might want to touch me again." Slowly, he raised his hand to his nose. "And your smell."

Ivy's face flamed.

"I don't believe I'll wash my hand for a great many hours. Maybe days."

She turned on her heel and walked away. When she reached the edge of the clearing, she called back to him, her words tight and clipped. "What happened to your binocs?"

"What?"

"Where are they? I didn't feel them when you were standing close to me."

"Oh. I just slung them in back."

"Oh."

"So it was lucky I bought a strap, instead of a harness."

Her voice came out waspish. "Well, don't blame me when you get a pinched nerve from carrying those heavy binoculars around, with all that weight dragging on your neck."

They reached the trailhead in silence.

"I can't use a binocular harness, Ivy. The strap catches the edge of the scar tissue."

She whirled around. "I'm sorry. I didn't think. I forgot."

"I didn't ignore your advice out of sheer cussedness."

She looked at his shoulders, wondering what his scars looked like, what they would feel like to touch. After several seconds, she realized that she was still staring and that he hadn't moved. She jerked her eyes up to his face.

He took a step, put his hands on her arms, bent his head, and closed his lips around the tip of her breast.

She gasped.

Hugh moved his mouth to her other breast, and then

slowly lifted his head. She looked down at the damp circles around her raised nipples.

"Why did you do that?"

"I thought they wanted attention."

Ivy stared at him in silence and then got in her car and slammed the door.

****

The mall corridors rang with the sounds of shop owners closing up for the night, rolling heavy metal gates across the fronts of their stores, calling out "goodbyes", exchanging short comments about evening plans. Ivy was closing her cash drawer when she saw Hugh striding toward her through the almost empty hall.

"I'm closing up."

"I want to ask you something."

"And it can't wait till tomorrow?"

"I want to know if there's anything we might do together."

Ivy frowned. "What kind of something?"

"Supper. Or a concert. A movie."

"Like a date?"

"Like a date. Yes."

"Oh." She looked down at her hands, still on the cash register. "Oh dear."

"Why? Why 'oh dear'?"

"I think, um, I've been thinking…" Ivy looked up, her eyes troubled and puzzled. "I think there are two different, um, possibilities, Hugh. Two different kinds of, or levels of, relationships we might, we might have. But one seems… it seems more plausible. To me. For us."

"Go on."

"If we, if we get together sometimes for birding but

occasionally, uh, we also, um, do what we did before…"
She took a deep breath and finished in a rush. "Then we
could be friends, I think. Friends who…"

Hugh jerked back from the counter. His normally
deep voice was almost a growl. "I did not come here to
suggest we get together to jerk each other off."

Ivy's words rushed together in her need to explain,
to erase the fierce look from his face. "No, no. I know
that. But I've thought about it. About the possibility of
being friends with you, sort of. Friends who give each
other some sexual excitement, or sexual fulfillment,
sometimes." She looked into his tight face, willing him
to understand. "But dating is different."

"Right. Dating is doing something together other
than jerking each other off. Dating is getting to know
each other."

Ivy stared at him mutely.

"Are you saying you have no interest in getting to
know me? But you might be interested in touching my
cock again sometime?"

"No! That's not… May I try to explain what I was
thinking?"

"Try. Do."

She took a deep breath and eased back so she could
sit on the stool behind the counter. "Okay. We've had
sex twice now." She expected him to interrupt, to qualify
her statement, to say 'sort of', but he remained quiet, his
dark eyes watching her. "But we haven't talked, at least
not a lot. We haven't kissed. We…" She hesitated. "We
haven't seen each other naked. So I think there's no
question that we're not lovers. Not really. So I had to
figure out what we are. What we are to each other. And
so that's why I came up with friends, friends who have

had sex twice. On a ledge and in a forest."

He didn't make quotation marks in the air but he didn't need to. She could hear the sarcasm when he spoke. "And you 'figured out' that's what we should remain? 'Friends' who might someday have more sex on ledges and in forests?"

"That's what… Yes."

He moved his head backwards and squinted as if trying to get her into focus. "Oh. Have you discovered that you get off on the outdoors thing? The possibility of being seen?"

"No!"

"Then why not think about having sex in a bed? In my bed, for example? Why not think about being what you call real lovers? What do you find so repugnant about that option?"

Ivy looked down at the counter. "It's not repugnant. You should know that."

"How? How would I know that you're not repulsed by the idea of being my lover? Of being naked with me? What clues have you given me? It's been weeks since the ledge, Ivy. In all that time, you've never voluntarily touched me, even in passing. You touch Jack and Charlie and Molly and Sean. Even Beck. But you take pains to avoid touching me. And you shy away if I even hint at touching you."

She didn't lift her head. His long fingers were gripping the edge of the counter. There was a narrow scar running along one index finger, and one knuckle had a tiny scratch.

"I e-mailed you two days ago, Ivy, to ask if you'd take a walk with me. You answered with four words. Four words. I'm. too. busy. Sorry."

Ivy was appalled to see two wet splotches on the counter and to feel tears sliding down her cheeks. "This is all going wrong. I thought I'd mention my idea about maybe having sex again and you'd be pleased."

Hugh's chest lifted with a deep breath. He took two steps back, let the breath out, and cleared his throat. "Ivy. I'm going to start this conversation over, from the start. All right?"

She nodded.

"First. I like the idea of having sex with you again. Of course. But that's not what I came here to ask you. Do you get that?"

"Yes."

"I came here to ask you on a date. Are you with me so far?"

She nodded again, staring down at the counter without seeing it.

"Good." He put both hands on the counter again and flexed his long fingers. His voice was tight and controlled. "All right. We're together to this point. Now. I'm going to restate what I think you've been saying. I'm doing so in the hope that you will hear how ridiculous it sounds. Will you listen?"

"You're starting from the premise that I'm ridiculous."

"Not you. What you're thinking right now. Will you hear me out?"

There was a brief pause before she nodded again.

"We have maintained emotional distance from each other, even with two satisfying sexual encounters. Is that right?"

"Yes."

"And I think that you believe emotional distance is

safe."

"Maybe."

"And you've 'figured out' that we might not be able to maintain emotional distance if we were to, say, sit across from each other in a restaurant, just the two of us, and talk. And get to know each other. Is that accurate?"

"Partly."

He took another deep breath. "Good. We're not completely at odds. I'm understanding what you're saying. Partly."

Hugh was quiet for so long that she almost looked up at him. But then he spoke again, his voice gentler than before. "And you're trying to make me believe that you want to be emotionally distant from me at the same time that you're crying because we're having an argument."

"I am not crying."

He reached up and touched her wet cheek. "And you believe that dating, getting to know each other better, might lead to all the rest. Being naked together. Caressing each other's bodies. Having intercourse. Having emotions. Being, in a word, lovers. And that scares you."

"Yes."

"Not repulses you. Scares you."

She looked up, her expression both defensive and belligerent. "Yes."

"Why? I'd be gentle, you know that by now. You don't have to be afraid about losing your virginity with me."

"It's not that. I *want*…" She stopped.

Hugh's expression had changed in an instant from puzzled to fiercely triumphant. "You've thought about losing your virginity with me."

"Of course I have. Duh."

"And you think you might want to."

She nodded.

"Then why…?"

"Oh, god." She knotted her hands together. "A very big part of me wants this conversation to be over and for you to get out of my shop." She felt around under the counter. "Do you have a tissue?"

He dug a handkerchief out of his pants pocket and handed it to her.

"But this must be important or I wouldn't be crying." She wiped her face and blew her nose. "I never cry."

He watched her wad up his handkerchief and throw it in the wastebasket.

"It's a stupid reason why I don't want to date you. It's because of later."

"When we're old and gray? That kind of later?"

"No. Later, when this relationship ends. If other people know we're together and then it, then it ends."

"That's somewhat ridiculous."

"No it isn't! Not to me. When this ends, everyone I know will feel sorry for me." She raised her tear-filled eyes. "I've already done the poor pitiful Ivy thing. For years! I wasn't married and wasn't even dating and every single person I knew thought there must be something wrong with me. I don't want to be pitied, ever again."

He reached out and covered her hands with his, holding them tightly when she tried to pull away. She looked down at their hands and gulped back tears.

"No one wants to be pitied, Ivy. I know that very well. Your emotion makes sense. But the reasoning behind the emotion is asinine."

"Great. I've progressed from ridiculous to asinine."

"Ivy, look at us. Look at the two of us. You're energetic, pretty, and well-liked. I'm a disillusioned grouch who smiles once a month, if that. I didn't have anyone even resembling a friend until I started birding. People in the BBC are sometimes afraid to talk to me. Right?"

She started to smile and made herself stop. "Sometimes. When you look all severe and disapproving."

"Which I often do. Right?"

"Yes."

"So just imagine how it will look if this disapproving and, and severe man begins following you around like a, like a hungry puppy. If he can't hide the fact that he gets a hard-on whenever he sees you."

"That's a bit of an exaggeration."

"It's not."

She started to say something more but he laid his fingertips against her mouth. "If people know we're dating, everyone will wonder what kind of magic you have. How you got through my thick crust of, of bitterness. And general negativity. And IF this relationship ends, every single person we know will feel sorry for me, for losing you. And they'll all figure that you got bored and dumped me."

Ivy mumbled something through her closed mouth and then reached up and moved his fingers away.

"I don't entirely believe that, Hugh."

"All right."

"But it was a very nice thing to say."

She studied his craggy face for a long moment.

"Do you have any place in mind? For this date?"

Chapter Nineteen

The vagrant balanced on the edge of the granite ledge, letting the sun warm its body after the chilly night. Far below, at the bottom of the cliff, a young moose walked by in awkward majesty. After it passed, each hoofprint slowly filled with tea-colored water, lined at the bottom with scores of tiny bubbles. The warbler watched the big animal until it ambled out of sight. Then it flew down to one of the new-made pools, dipped its bill and drank.

Chapter Twenty

"This was a very smart idea for a first date."

"Thank you. Why?"

"A museum gave us built-in things to talk about."

The afternoon was hot, with a soft breeze that played with their hair and tugged at their clothes as they strolled across the broad lawn.

"You think we wouldn't have had anything to talk about if we'd done something different?"

"Maybe. But we might have been reduced to favorite colors and what's your middle name."

At his car, they opened all the doors and stood outside, waiting for the breeze to cool the inside.

"Tan. Finley," he said.

"Tan? Your favorite color is tan? That's exceptionally bland."

"It was the first thing that popped into my mind."

"Oh."

"And you always wear tan, on bird walks."

"Oh."

"You?"

"Me what?"

He sighed. "Your favorite color. Your middle name."

"Oh. Blue, I guess. And Artemesia. Believe it or not."

The corner of his mouth twisted up. "Artemesia?

Your parents looked down at an innocent little baby and thought, 'Let's name her Ivy Artemesia'?"

"Ivy Artemesia Pritchard. Has quite a ring to it."

"Did they hate you or something?"

Her blue eyes met his. "Maybe. Quite possibly, actually."

He frowned and opened his mouth to ask another question but Ivy was now looking past him, intent and excited.

"Whoa! That's not a Ring-billed."

"What?"

"That one gull. Look. They're all the same size, Ring-billed Gulls, except for the one on the near end."

Hugh slowly moved his eyes from her face to the gulls at the edge of the parking lot. "So what is it?"

"Bonaparte's. A Bonaparte's Gull. See the black behind the eye? A few weeks ago, the whole head would have been black."

"Breeding plumage?"

"Yes."

Even without binoculars, they could easily distinguish the one petite gull from the others.

"Named for the emperor?"

"The emperor's nephew. A naturalist, in Philadelphia or some place."

All the gulls took to the air as a school bus turned into the parking lot.

"I didn't expect to add a bird to my life list at the museum."

"Birds everywhere. So many birds." Ivy got into the car. "We can still leave the doors open for a while."

"All right."

She looked out through the windshield at the

140

buildings scattered here and there on the museum's sloping lawn, the glinting lake in the far background. She sat tall and straight, knotting her hands together in her lap. "This was a good idea."

"So you said."

"Very diverse."

"Yes."

"History and art and, and more history."

"Yes."

"And also I've lived in Vermont my whole life but I've only been here once. Back in grade school. It was good to see it with someone who has curiosity and, and stamina."

He was watching her with a quizzical expression. "It *is* huge."

She swallowed. "Damn. I'm too old to be this nervous."

"Why are you nervous?"

She looked at him, her eyes embarrassed but also helplessly amused. "I want this date to end with a kiss."

"At least."

"So I'm going to be a nervous wreck, waiting the whole drive home."

"We could do a first kiss now. Here."

"Oh."

"Get it over with."

"That's a, that's a good idea."

"Given that we've been sneaking glances at each other's mouths since lunch."

Ivy shook her head. "Longer than that."

"Oh?"

"First thing this morning, in the tool barn. When you and that guy were talking about those two-man saws."

"Bucking and felling."

"Beg pardon?"

"There were two-man bucking saws and two-man felling saws."

"Oh. I couldn't stop watching your mouth. W—"

She stopped abruptly when he ran his finger along her lower lip.

"Wanting?"

"I was going to say wondering. But wanting, yes. That too."

He caressed her upper lip.

She spoke against his fingertips. "Twice now, Hugh. Twice in my life, I thought I knew what a man wanted. But I was wrong both times. Completely wrong."

Hugh put his hands on her shoulders and leaned back, pushing her away the full length of his arms. "You're going to talk. Aren't you?"

She shrugged.

"You're going to talk while I'm kissing you. You're going to talk all the time we're making love."

Ivy's whole body was suddenly washed with a hot tingling sensation. "I'm sorry. I, I might talk too much just to… I don't want to misunderstand anything. I want to make sure I'm not having one experience, and expecting one thing, and then find out you're on an entirely different, um, planet or something."

Hugh slowly shook his head, his brown eyes uncharacteristically gentle.

"What?" Ivy scowled at him. "You think that's not possible? I'm telling you. It is."

"We are a pitiful duo."

"What?"

"Pitiful and laughable. You're going to keep talking

because you're afraid we might not be on the same planet. The same page, anyway. And I'm worried that maybe you keep talking because we're not."

"Not?"

"On the same page. On the same planet. Right now, for instance. I'm wondering if you're stalling, finding excuses not to have this kiss."

"I'm not. I think I'm going to very much like kissing you."

He looked solemn, frowning slightly. Then he leaned closer. She felt the touch of his moustache and then his lips against hers. He leaned back to watch her face again.

"Not enough, Hugh."

He kissed her again, barely touching her with his lips, feather-light pressure lifted immediately, followed by another and another.

Ivy held her breath. She wanted to watch his face and also to close her eyes. She wanted to feel his light kisses forever and also to have him kiss her harder. When his mouth touched hers again and he didn't pull away, she slid her hand into the thick hair at the nape of his neck and let her eyes drift closed. Finally, finally, she felt his tongue and met it with her own. She heard him groan and felt it in her mouth and chest.

After minutes that seemed very long to Ivy, and not nearly long enough, Hugh put his hands on both sides of her head and leaned back.

"Stop. For now."

She reached up and traced his mouth with her fingertips. "You have a very beautiful mouth. That's what I kept thinking this morning."

"At the tool exhibit."

"Yes. With the, um, bucking and felling saws."

His lips twitched.

"Are you laughing at me?"

"Yes." He ran long fingers into her hair. "And I expect to do so again. It feels good."

"But it… Laughing is fine but I think kissing might be better."

"Later." He turned away from her and slammed his door. "In private. Your door."

"Oh." She pulled her door closed and put on her seatbelt and then waited, confused, when he just sat and looked out the windshield.

"One more thing, Ivy."

"What?"

"It's okay if you talk." He glanced over at her. "You can talk while we're kissing. You can check in with me every step of the way, to make sure we're on the same page. You can talk while we're making love. You can recite the Gettysburg Address. You can sing, loudly. The whole score of *Oliver*, if that's what you want. We'll close the bedroom window so we don't alarm or confound the neighbors."

Ivy felt herself starting to grin. "I think that singing all of *Oliver* would require more concentration than I'll have to spare."

She remembered thinking, back when Hugh came on his first FATSO walk, how cold his eyes were, how distant and measuring and judging and cold. Now his eyes were alive with heat.

"Which one of our houses? Mine is nearer."

She was so absorbed in watching the play of sunlight on his face that she almost forgot she didn't have a house to take him to.

"Oh. Yours."

Ivy saw the sudden flare of excitement on his face and felt an answering excitement in her belly. He turned away, fumbling with the key. "This is going to be the longest forty-something miles of my entire life."

As he pulled out of the parking lot, she reached up and touched his jaw, his ear.

"It's not safe for you to do that." He shot her a look out of the corner of his eye. "I need at least a little blood getting to my brain. For driving."

She glanced down at his lap and then made herself look away. "Should I turn on your radio?"

"No. Talk to me. What kind of music do you like?"

"Many different things."

"Specifics."

"Well. Seventies and eighties rock, for when I'm doing something that takes time and energy but no mental activity."

"Like what?"

"Like taking everything off the shelves in the shop and dusting and putting everything back."

"Like what groups? Give me some names."

"SuperTramp. Styx. Journey."

"Don't know them." He concentrated on merging onto the highway and then asked, "Why seventies and eighties? You were just a baby."

"The nearest cottage to my tree house—"

Hugh looked over at her, startled.

"—belonged to a couple who played that kind of music all the time."

"Tree house?"

"I used to live in a commune. In a tree house."

"The commune. Yes. You mentioned that before."

The old Audi purred as Hugh got up to highway speed. "Whole story there. Let's save it for another time. Next date."

Ivy tilted her head back and let the wind tangle her mop of dark curls, watching the flex of tendons and muscles under the skin of his hands as he pulled out and passed a slow-moving van. Then she looked out the window without seeing the traffic or the beautifully designed median with wildflowers and little clusters of trees, or the farm fields, or the occasional rock ledges on the sides of the road.

"This is all new to me."

"I-89? It's won awards for the most scenic interstate in the east."

"Not the interstate." She twisted in her seat to face him. "I don't think you realize what a limited life I've had."

He looked over at her, his face solemn. "Are you having second thoughts?"

"Absolutely not."

"Are you still a nervous wreck?"

"No. Surprisingly, no. Not anymore." Ivy reached out and ran her fingers along his jaw. "I'm feeling anticipation. Not anxiety."

Hugh took her hand and rested their joined hands on her thigh. "That is very good, Ivy."

"But I was just realizing that this is the first time in my life I've been in a car with a man I have kissed and want to kiss a lot more."

She watched the shape of his mouth change from a line to a curve.

"And that makes me tingly."

"Tingly. That's good."

"I was also thinking that we got to know each other better today."

"I agree."

"Today felt very personal."

"I agree again. And?"

"I have no experience being personal with a man."

He shot her an exasperated look. "It didn't feel personal when you held my cock in your hands? It didn't feel personal when I made you come with my fingers? I felt your body stiffen and strain and then shudder and go limp against me. That felt very personal to me."

She tried to ignore the sudden heat, the sudden dampness in her palms and between her legs. "I don't know how to describe it, Hugh, but those moments felt out-of-time. Out-of-reality. I was so caught up in sensations, what was happening to me." She looked at his profile, his straight nose, the short neat beard and mustache, the chin that was so often lifted aggressively. "But today I was paying attention to you. So I know you much better after today than I did after those other times."

"Oh. You put that very clearly. I'm sorry I snapped at you."

"Feeling personal about you feels different from my other friendships. With, say, Molly or Jack. Or Charlie or Sean."

She saw the flash of his smile, very white between his beard and mustache.

"I fervently hope so."

****

Hugh let the car roll down his driveway and braked in front of the garage door. He unfastened his seatbelt but made no move to get out.

"Before we go in."

"Yes?"

"I initiated both of the two times we had sex. And I touched you first this afternoon, in the car at the museum. I kissed you first."

"I was right there, Hugh. I wasn't objecting. Not any of those times."

"But the fact remains that we might never have touched, at all, if it had been up to you. Before we go in, I need you to make a first move."

"I have no idea how to go about seducing you."

He turned his head and looked at her. "Well, one, I don't think it would be a good idea for you to seduce me out here, with the neighbors having a barbecue just a few yards away. And, two, I'm not looking for slinky negligees or, uh, pole dancing."

"Good. Pole dancing is outside my comfort zone."

"Is telling people what you're thinking inside your comfort zone?"

Ivy looked at his tense and anxious face and felt herself beginning to relax. "Hah. Just ask any member of the BBC."

"Then tell me what you were thinking, all the way home. What you're thinking now." He touched her face but immediately withdrew his hand. "Chalk it up to bruised self-confidence. I need a strong hit of assurance that you really want to come inside with me."

"Well. First. While you were driving. I was thinking that you have a very nice nose. Noble."

"Noble nose. What else?"

"And I kept watching your hands, on the steering wheel. And," she cleared her throat, "I was thinking that, in just a little while, when we get back to your house, I'd be feeling those hands all over me. Without clothes."

She leaned closer. "And right after you started driving, before we even got out of the parking lot, I was thinking that I'd like to feel your beard against my skin. Lots of men have scraggly, sparse beards. A few hairs here and there." She caressed his jaw with her cheek. "Yours is like fur."

She touched her lips to his neck. "And I was thinking that I might want to kiss you here."

She felt him swallow.

"And then I was studying your ear."

"My ear."

"I missed the whole Bolton Flats area, Hugh. I didn't see any of it because I was looking at your ear. I've never kissed anybody's ear but it suddenly seemed like an excellent thing to do."

She took his head in her hands and turned his face toward the windshield. "I kept thinking about doing this." She kissed the top of his ear and then the side and then his earlobe. "And this." She ran the tip of her tongue all around the edge and then, quickly, dipped in and out.

Hugh made a noise deep in his throat and she saw him clench his hands on the steering wheel, the knuckles white against his tan. His voice was almost a croak. "That's… that's quite reassuring."

Ivy felt a tingling rush of power and anticipation. "That was a long drive. I did a lot of thinking. I'm not done telling you about it."

"Oh god."

"All that thinking made me…" She searched for the right word. "Molten."

"Out."

"Pardon?"

"Get out."

They'd walked only a few yards toward the house when he stopped, his fingers tightening around hers almost painfully.

"What's the matter? Are we locked out?"

He tilted his head up and drew a long shuddering breath. "Do you... Are you going to want a drink? Coffee?"

"What?"

"A snack? A tour of the house?"

"No. None of those."

"Can we go straight through to the bedroom?"

"Yes."

"Thank god."

****

Ivy got a quick impression of a large square foyer, a kitchen to the right, and a long hall with skylights. Then they were at his bedroom.

"Hugh, wait."

He stopped dead. "What? What, Ivy? What?"

"It was a hot day, and I'm... I feel sweaty. And icky."

"Oh. Yes. Me too."

"I'd like to take a shower before... first?"

"Oh. Yes. Of course." He put his hands on her shoulders and turned her. "You use the master bath. In here. I'll use the guest bath. We'll meet here in five minutes? Yes?"

"Yes."

"Ivy?"

She turned back toward him. "Yes?"

"Can we not... Is it all right with you if we don't put any clothes back on?"

"Oh. Okay. Yes."

****

The bedroom was empty when Ivy came back. She wanted a towel or a blanket to wrap around herself, but she also wanted to be naked for him.

She was very aware of his bed. Lots of people had king-sized beds. But Hugh's bed looked implausibly large, acres and acres of off-white bedspread.

What if he'd changed his mind? What if he'd decided he didn't want to make love with her? What if—

Then he was there.

"Hi."

"Hi."

"I think we should get into bed."

"Yes."

Hugh threw back the covers and Ivy scrambled onto the huge bed and reached for him.

As soon as his mouth covered hers, the rising anxiety was over. It was the same as in the museum parking lot, only so much better. He was warm and real and solid, warm skin stretched over bones and muscles, rough hair on arms and legs and chest. She was giddy with the realization that there wouldn't be any stopping, that he was her first lover, that they were making love here in his huge bed.

After many minutes, Hugh raised his head and met her eyes and then bent again and kissed her forehead, her cheeks, the corners of her mouth, her chin. When he angled his head to put his lips on her neck, she made a sound that was part sigh and part moan.

"This is… new, to me, but it doesn't feel new. I don't know why."

She felt his smile against her shoulder.

"We do have some history, Ivy."

"Oh. Yes. That must be it."

He leaned up on one arm, watching his fingers trace a path along the slopes of her breasts. "I've kissed you here before." He bent his head and put his mouth around one taut nipple and then the other.

"Oh. Yes." Her voice was shaky, whispery. "It feels better without my shirt."

"For me too."

He opened his mouth and touched her with his tongue, caressing and tasting and kissing. She made a little noise and burrowed her fingers through his thick hair to the hard warm scalp, holding him closer. Her entire being was concentrated on the different sensations from his lips, tongue, mustache, and beard. On the little pulling kisses he was placing all around her breasts, under, on the sides, between.

On his warm hard hand moving back and forth above her belly and then back and forth lower.

Hugh raised his mouth just a little and she felt the resonance of his deep voice in her chest. "We've done this before too."

She gave a breathless laugh. "Right."

She spread her legs without knowing she did it. She felt his finger and knew she was slick and wet, knew he would think she was ready. She wasn't sure she was but she didn't want to wait much longer. She moaned as his finger slid into her. Then two fingers, gently stretching.

"This feels… I think… Hugh. I want you in me."

He reached across her and opened a drawer in the nightstand. "Condoms."

"Yes." She looked at the little pile he dropped onto the bed beside her. "That's quite a few."

"Yes."

She watched him roll the condom down.

"Next time I'd love it if you'd do this. But right now your fingers on me would end things."

She spread her legs and he knelt between and then took both of her ankles and brought them close to her bottom. When he rose over her, she grabbed his rigid arms, her fingers tight around tight muscles. She felt blunt thickness against her, and then pressure, and then sudden slipping entry.

"I'm in you."

"Yes."

"More?"

"Yes. Yes, please."

He moved until he felt resistance, then out, and in. She sighed and ran her hands up and down his arms, watching his taut face. It felt as if many minutes passed, many minutes of Hugh's slow movements, many minutes of breathless waiting.

"Hugh? Please."

"I've been trying to get past. This might hurt, Ivy." He lifted a shaking hand and brushed her hair off her forehead. "But I think only for a second. Hug me with your legs."

"Pardon?"

"Put your legs up around my hips."

She had barely lifted her feet off the bed when he thrust hard. She gasped and stiffened, her legs awkwardly in the air, her eyes tightly closed, her fingers biting into his arms. He thrust again, and then stopped moving for a long moment before pulling out very slowly.

When he pressed back in even more slowly, Ivy

lowered her legs around his back and he let out a long breath. "Open your eyes. I'm coming all the way in now."

"Oh god. I thought…"

She felt impossibly stretched, impossibly filled.

For long moments, they moved slowly, her hips rising with every slow entrance. His arms shook under her tight fingers. He started moving faster and she tried to match his motions but she couldn't.

"Next time will be better, Ivy. I can't… Oh, god."

And she heard for the second time the noise he'd made when they were on the ledge.

****

Hugh pulled away and reached across her to drop the condom in the wastebasket. When he lowered his head and pressed little kisses along the side of her neck, Ivy breathed a long sigh.

"We're not done?"

"Done?" His lips and mustache tickled the side of her breast.

"I didn't know… I thought maybe you would… And I barely started touching you." She flexed her fingers. "I didn't know what to do with my hands." She felt him smile. "Is there any place you'd rather not be touched?"

Hugh leaned up on one arm. "There is absolutely nowhere you can't touch me, Ivy. And we are absolutely not done."

"I'm very happy to hear that, Hugh."

There were two patches of burn scar, one making a hairless S-shape just above his nipple and the other, much larger, capping his shoulder. She closed her eyes briefly and then, aware that he was watching, opened them again and tentatively slid both hands up and over

154

his shoulders. The hard, smooth burn scar extended down to cover his shoulder blade.

"You don't have to be afraid to touch me there."

"You're sure?"

"I'm sure." He closed his eyes. "This is the first time anyone has ever touched me there. Except for doctors and nurses."

Ivy briefly tightened her fingers and then stroked his shoulders, the one so warm and supple and the other so different. After many minutes, she slid her hands down his back to his cool buttocks and then around his waist and up again to the dark red hairs on his chest. He sucked in a harsh breath when her fingers touched a hard brown nipple.

"You're sensitive here?"

"God yes."

She leaned up and touched him with her tongue.

"Oh God, yes."

Her legs moved restlessly against his, feeling the rough hairs and long runner's muscles. She felt his foot against her calf and let him spread her legs apart. He smoothed his hand down her body and again parted her tight black curls.

"Hugh."

"Mmm?"

"Just Hugh." Her head fell back and her eyes closed. "Hugh!"

****

When she was able to breathe again, and to focus, he had another of the bright-colored packets in his hand.

"Please?"

She sat up and took it from him.

"This is incredibly sexy, Ivy. You're getting me

ready to be inside you."

"Yes."

Then he was kneeling between her legs again, and this time she hugged him with her legs from the very beginning. His eyes were dark with heat but he was smiling a little, and he teased them both by stopping only a little way in and moving just a centimeter in and out and in and out. She reached up and caressed his face and smiled back at him. When he started a strong regular rhythm of thrust and retreat, her hips rose and fell with him.

"We're doing it, Hugh."

"Eh?"

"We're doing it this time." She tightened her hands on his buttocks. "That's what it feels like. Like we're doing it."

He looked down at her quizzically. "We weren't a few minutes ago?"

"Before it felt like you were doing it. Now *we*'re doing it." She pressed her hands against his bottom and slid her legs a little further up his back. "And I'm talking. Is that okay?"

"I would not have expected anything else."

****

"I feel sorry for your wife."

He jerked his hand away from her breast. "I thought... You... I'm sorry."

Ivy lifted her head and looked down at him, astonished. "You are not a moron! So don't act like one! I *loved* what we just did. You know I did! You heard all the moaning and gasping!" She guided his hand back to her breast. "I feel sorry for your wife because if she didn't realize that being in bed with you is truly wonderful, then there was something seriously wrong with her."

He circled her nipple with his fingertips. "You have nothing to compare me with."

"I've been reading romance novels for decades now." She looked down at his hand on her breast and traced the skin between his fingers. "I can knowledgeably compare you to the heroes of about five hundred books."

"Goody." He lifted his hand, put both arms under his head and stretched out his full length. "Go for it."

"Well, Hugh." Ivy rested her head on his shoulder and watched his profile. "The foreplay was gentle, thoughtful. Effective."

"Foreplay was pretty much all day long." He raised an eyebrow in her direction. "Even before your surprising moves out in the car."

"It was, wasn't it? All day. I kept… I slowed down every time we got to a door so you'd put your hand on my back. Did you notice?"

"No."

"And when we were walking back to the car, I wanted to touch your hand, to have us hold hands." She ran her fingers over his chest, barely touching the soft curls, enjoying the tickling feeling.

"Next date, please follow your instincts."

She gave a breathless little laugh. "Some of them anyway."

"Oh."

She turned her head and kissed his shoulder. "And once we got to bed, the foreplay got even better. You were cautious of my ignorance, but you also recognized that I really…" She swallowed. "Really didn't want to wait." Her eyes and her fingers followed his chest hair as it narrowed at his waist and then flared again. "And intercourse wasn't over in a matter of seconds..."

"The first time didn't last long."

"But the first time was followed, after a brief interlude, by the second time." She smiled against the warm skin of his shoulder. "And the interlude featured an extravagantly wonderful orgasm, for me. And then there was the third time, and that was extraordinary." She trailed her fingers back and forth across his belly, watching in fascination as the muscles tightened in response. "And I think you have more than adequate length and, um, diameter."

He made a stifled noise and she watched his chest and belly quaking.

"You think that's a laughing matter? I assure you, it's considered very important in books. No matter what we hear about size not counting, an illogical percentage of romance novel heroes are above average. Often the female protagonists gasp in awe and trepidation."

She felt his silent laughter again. "I'm new at this, Hugh, but I'm wondering if all the guffawing is a good sign."

"Chuckling, Ivy. Not guffawing." He straightened his right arm and pulled her close. "Chuckling in bed—for that matter, any lightness or happiness in bed—hasn't been part of my life for a very long time." He stroked her rib cage, her waist, her hip. "The important question is how did my, uh, length and diameter *feel*? Are you sore?"

"No. I'm not sore. But it was a huge feeling, Hugh. I had no idea. It felt like you were in every single part of my body."

"Ivy."

"Every single atom."

For long minutes, there was only his mouth on hers, his tongue, his taste. She couldn't even caress him. She couldn't move. There was nothing but their mouths.

Finally he lifted his head and looked down at her. She watched his slow smile and felt its mirror image widen her own mouth. He lay back down, still smiling, and she slid her thigh over his and her arm around his waist.

"Back to my comparison between you and romance heroes." She traced the taut skin between his ribs. "Believe me, Hugh. If this past hour or so were written up in a novel, every woman who read it would get horny. Your wife must have been either nuts or stupid."

He made a sound like a grunt, but the corner of his mouth tipped up.

"Hugh?"

"Mmm?"

"Part of me wishes I'd been doing this for years and years, having sex. Like any normal woman. That I hadn't wasted so much of my life not knowing what this feels like. But part of me is glad because, if I'd known what to expect, I might not have been so blown away today."

"I'm glad you were blown away. I was too." He dropped a kiss on her breast and then abruptly sat up. "I'm ravenous. I'm going to make us an omelet. Then I want us to come back to bed."

"Yes."

Chapter Twenty-One

"Hugh?" She looked at him over the rim of her coffee mug. "You bought a great many condoms."

"This is true."

"I was just thinking that we shouldn't... That we might not need any more of them."

He became very still, a piece of toast in one hand and a knife in the other. "I was very much hoping we would."

"No! I didn't mean... I mean, we can have sex without them. Can't we?"

His dark eyes searched hers.

"I've never had sex before. And you haven't for years. So we don't have to worry about, about diseases. Unless you have some chronic something, from before."

"I don't."

"And I..." She could feel herself blushing. "I started taking birth control pills back in May."

"You hadn't before?"

"No."

"Why did you start?"

The color in her cheeks darkened. "There was no point, most of my life. And then you... It looked like you would be a regular on FATSO walks. When I had my annual check-up and she asked if there was any possibility I might be, might be sexually active anytime soon, I..." She raised one shoulder in a little shrug. "I didn't *expect*... But just in case."

In slow motion, Hugh laid the knife on his plate and lowered the piece of toast. "I have been quite successfully focusing on eggs and toast and coffee, with you sitting only a few feet away with nothing on under my robe. But now I can't think of anything except being inside you naked." He pushed his plate away. "I've never done that before, Ivy. Never."

"Not even when you were married?"

"Elaine was terrified of getting pregnant. She was on the pill but we used condoms anyway. She even used a diaphragm for a while too." His mouth twisted in a humorless smile. "She really didn't want my child."

"I'm sorry."

"I was too, for a while. But I'm glad we didn't have children. As it turned out."

She looked down his long bare torso. "Are you hard?"

"Getting there."

"Show me."

He pushed his chair back and stood up. Watching her face, he untied the cord of his sweat pants, lifted the waistband out and over, pushed the sweatpants to his thighs and let them drop.

"Amazing."

She didn't see the red stain across his cheekbones.

"What an amazing system. Seeing you like that makes me, um, melt. I think even my bones just got soft." She looked up. "Your body changes because of me, and my body changes because of you."

"Bed."

Ivy stood up and Hugh reached out and pulled one end of her belt. When the robe fell open, she shrugged out of it and dropped it on top of his sweat pants.

****

At first, she was impatient with his slow pace, but then she began to feel as if he was reaching up into her whole torso.

Slow entrance, stretching her, widening her. Even slower withdrawal.

Again and again and again. She was sure she could feel him behind her breasts, taste him low in her throat.

Without warning, Hugh's control snapped. One second they were moving together in slow motion, watching each other's faces, both smiling a little. The next second his body was heavy against hers, pressing her into the bed, his chin hard against her temple, his hips pumping with a desperate, frantic, uneven rhythm that she couldn't match.

She felt startled, almost giggly. But as it went on and on, she began to feel distant from the laboring, grunting man on top of her.

Fucking. The word came into her mind. This is what people meant. Hugh was blindly, mindlessly fucking. It came to her that she would have been frightened if it had happened a few hours earlier. But now she wasn't. Now she was lying under him being fucked and she wasn't afraid because now she was what she hadn't been that morning. Now she was a normal woman who knew something about sex, a woman who was no longer a virgin.

Her whole body was suddenly flooded with a wave of gratitude and affection, and the feeling of being distant from him disappeared. She flexed her fingers down the length of his sweat-slicked back and writhed under him, sliding her legs a little higher, trying to get him even deeper. A heavy ache bloomed in her belly and grew.

The relentless, almost mechanical pumping continued. Now she was breathing as fast and as harshly as he was. The feeling in her belly became painful, and she began to feel that she needed his orgasm as much as he did.

Hugh moved his head and she felt his clenched teeth hard against her forehead. Then he went rigid, his whole body stretched and straining, every bit of him still, except his throbbing, pulsing sex. And Ivy sucked in a moaning gasp and convulsed around him.

There were no sounds but their gradually slowing breaths and the gradually quieting thunder of their hearts. After a long moment, he raised his head.

"Are you all right?"

Ivy's body was wracked by a shuddering aftershock. She felt emptied, incapable of thought, without words. She came out with a whispered "wonderful".

"Yes. Wonderful."

She felt his legs tense, his torso lift.

"Don't. Not yet."

"I'm too heavy for you."

"No. Don't."

In slow motion, she lowered her legs to the bed and he lay back down on her, their bodies touching from feet to head. She stroked his long back, feeling the different textures: his hard cool shoulder and his warm flexible shoulder, the ridge of his spine, the stretched smooth skin. Barely moving, her fingertips traced the tight creases at the top of his thighs and then started back up, this time stroking the moist valley between his buttocks.

His torso jerked in a little laugh.

"What?"

"The way you're touching me right now…"

"Yes?"

"If I weren't completely wiped…" Another gasping laugh. "What you're doing right now would get me very hot very fast."

"Oh. That's good to know. For the future."

After, when she wanted very much to relive every minute, Ivy found that she had no idea how long they lay in his big bed, their racing hearts quieting, her hands lazily exploring.

Hugh's long body went slack, his breathing deepened, and she realized that he was asleep. She lay awake under him, full of a shimmering wonder. She was astonished that he had fallen asleep with part of him still inside her. This was Hugh. Hugh from the bird walks. And now he was sleeping with his penis inside her.

She was touched at the thought of his tired penis resting in her soft warmth. Would his penis be tired? She didn't know. Maybe not. His hips and legs had been doing all the work.

Perhaps fifteen minutes passed, maybe a half hour, before his body tightened, before there was less weight against her.

"I was asleep."

She moved her hand to the side of his neck. "You were."

"I'm still in you."

"You are."

"I've never… You must be almost flattened." He pushed himself up on his arms. She felt him slide out of her, and he rolled to his back.

"I was going to wake you up in a few minutes." She sat up. "Hugh?"

"Mmmm?"

"I don't think any woman in the history of the world has had a first time so… This has been glorious, Hugh."

She felt his warm hand on the small of her back.

"I don't think any man in all of history has had a time like this. Ever."

Hugh exerted just the least bit of pressure on her back and she eagerly lowered her head for a gentle, long, slow, deep kiss. When she sat up again, her eyes were satiny with tears.

"I'll be right back."

When she finished in the bathroom, he was asleep again. She walked all the way around the big bed and crawled across it, stopping to free the sheet from under his feet so she could pull it over them. He turned onto his side when she lay down, pulling her closer, and they fell asleep facing each other, their heads on the same pillow.

****

Ivy stood by the wide bedroom window, wrapped in Hugh's blue shirt from the day before. Morning sun filled the room with pale gold light. Outside, two cement walls many yards long and many feet high provided privacy for a little patio. At the far end, birches and willows were hung with bird feeders. A pair of binoculars lay on a little table just inside the window.

His voice came from the bed behind her, deep and raspy and slow. "I never had bird feeders before this house."

She turned, smiling. "Good morning."

"Yes. It is." He sat up. "The best I've had in… Well, ever."

"Me too."

"Don't move. I'll be right back."

Ivy watched him get out of bed and head for the bathroom, and then she waited, facing the patio with unfocused eyes, smiling.

"You found a new toothbrush. Good."

"You're well-equipped with extras."

He joined her at the window. "Did you think about using mine?"

"Pardon?"

"My toothbrush."

"Oh. I did, actually. Think about it. But I decided that might be something about which polite lovers should ask first."

"Polite lovers, huh?" He touched her cheek. "The etiquette of being lovers."

"Yes."

"It would have been fine. Nice even."

"Good to know."

"Let's do a proper good morning. Like polite lovers."

The kiss was minty and gentle and long.

"I like you in my shirt." He kissed her again. "Get rid of it."

"Pardon?"

"My shirt. Ditch it."

"Oh."

Ivy undid the buttons and dropped the shirt to the floor.

"Much better." He looked at her from chin to knees, sighed, and hugged her to his side.

"Hugh?"

"Mmm?"

"I like looking at your body too. When you got out of bed and walked to the bathroom, I was thinking that

I'd like to lie in bed sometime, with you here at the window, and spend some time just looking."

"A butt woman, huh?"

"I don't think so. I like looking at your front too." Her face and neck immediately flooded with heat. "But your bottom is so nice and tight. It's lovely."

"Lovely."

"Yes. It's…" She searched for the right words. "It's just a perfect connector between your wonderful long torso and your beautiful long legs."

"You're… I'm feeling more than a little embarrassed."

She slid her arm around his waist, leaning close to feel his rough warmth against her breast. "And I like the fact that it's not all hairy. One of the men at the commune was, well, he wasn't furry exactly, but he had maybe a hundred wavy black hairs on his butt. Each one at least an inch long. He was a nice man, and sort of attractive when he was dressed, but in the hot tub he was quite repulsive."

"So. What have you been seeing?"

"Pardon?"

"At my feeders."

"Oh. Birds. Well, Black-capped Chickadees. White-breasted Nuthatches. Well, only one nuthatch. A glorious male cardinal. A few Chipping Sparrows. Two Tufted Titmice."

"Titmice nested in an old woodpecker hole in one of the big oaks at the back of my property. They fledged four young."

"Excellent." Ivy looked into Hugh's face, her eyes puzzled. "I didn't notice the feeders at all yesterday. Or the fact that this whole wall is glass, something that should have been very hard to miss."

A corner of his mouth quirked up. "I find that very gratifying. That *you* didn't notice birds."

"I was distracted."

"So, what else?"

"Pardon?"

"What other birds?"

"Oh." She looked through the window again. "Okay. There's a catbird lurking in that viburnum or whatever it is. And a Carolina Wren on the ground."

Hugh's head jerked up. "A Carolina Wren? Where?"

Ivy picked up the binoculars from the little table and handed them to him. "Creeping around under the feeder that's in the birch. It's partially hidden but… there! Now it's in the open. Like a stealthy little mouse."

"I've seen this bird before but never well enough or long enough to ID it."

They both watched as the little brown bird hopped back and forth in the leaf litter, repeatedly raising and lowering its tail.

Hugh turned his head and slowly smiled. "A life list bird before breakfast. A totally unnecessary addition to an already perfect morning."

"Excellent."

"Why are you up so early, anyway?"

"This is my usual time. I would have loved to stay cuddled in bed this morning, but I feel… I feel electrified. Wired. I had to get up or I would have started vibrating or thrashing around or something."

He looked at the clock next to the bed. "When do you have to be at work?"

"Omigosh. Work. I completely forgot this is a

regular workday."

The slow smile softened his face again, lighting up his dark eyes. "Again, I'm gratified."

"The mall opens at ten. I should be there by 9:45 at the latest."

"You have to go all the way home to get clothes, though."

"No. I, um, I have a change at the shop."

He glanced at the clock again and then met her eyes. "That being the case, we have lots of time. I suggest that we return to bed for an hour or so. And then I'll make breakfast while you shower and get ready. Then I'll drive you to get your car. And after work, you'll join me here for supper." His voice deepened. "And spend the night again."

"I like that plan."

They turned away from the window, toward the rumpled bed.

"Hugh?"

"Eh?"

"You're not thinking that we should go back to bed to catch up on sleep, are you?"

"Not for anything in the world."

"Excellent."

****

"This is ridiculous," Ivy muttered. "To use his favorite word." She picked up her office phone, irritated to see that her hand was shaking. "I am a full-grown woman. I am not fifteen."

"Did you say something, Ivy?"

Ivy looked up to see Molly's face peering around the edge of the door. "No. Sorry. Just talking to myself."

She'd been talking to herself for several minutes,

sternly. She'd reminded herself how wonderful the afternoon and night had been. And the morning. How he had wanted her again and again. How much she'd wanted him, every time. She'd reminded herself how comfortable they'd been together after sex, how easily they'd talked while they were eating the omelet he'd made for supper and this morning's pancakes, how warm his eyes had been when he asked her to have supper with him and spend the night again.

But the fact remained that she had never in her life called a man about a date.

"Oh! I thought I'd get a machine. Do you work at home?"

"My office is here. In the house." She thought she could hear a smile in his voice. "Maybe tonight we'll get around to a tour."

"I'm just… I called to ask what I can bring."

"I'm cooking, remember?"

"I know, but I should bring something. Dessert. Appetizer. Something."

"Ivy, I used to cook all the time, and I liked it. I got out of the habit when it was just me. I'm looking forward to cooking for two. Besides, you said you don't cook."

"Well, I could."

"I'm sure you could. But not tonight." His deep voice deepened. "Just you. Just bring you. As soon as possible."

"Okay." Ivy was suddenly breathless. "Right after the shop closes."

She had barely put the phone down when it rang.

"Ivy's Optics and Accessories for the…"

"Half-and-half."

"Beg pardon?"

"I'm almost out of half-and-half. You could bring some."

A grin spread over her face. "Oh. Yes. I'll bring half-and-half."

Ivy put the phone down and let her fingers slide off in slow motion. When she looked up, Molly was watching her again, her eyes interested and curious.

"Oh! Molly! I was thinking about the inventory. Do you remember if we ordered extra copies of that new shorebird guide?"

****

"Do you read mysteries?"

Ivy looked up from her computer. "Rarely. Why?"

"I do. All the time. So I'm pleased to have solved one on my own."

"Murder in the Montpelier Mall?"

Molly plopped down on Ivy's daybed with one leg folded under her. "Not a murder mystery. A happy-making mystery. Here are the clues. One." She made her eyes wide. "Your lips are swollen."

Ivy pushed her chair back from the desk.

"Two. I see what appears to be a love nip on the left side of your neck. Three. I just heard you sighing 'half-and-half' like it was some sort of magic incantation, and at the same time you were petting the phone." Molly pretended to look puzzled and concerned. "Very peculiar behavior, Ivy. Alarming even."

Ivy started to smile. "So. Detective Molly. What's your solution to this mystery?"

"That you spent the night with some studly dude. A very good night, based on the glazed look in your eyes."

Ivy took a deep breath. "I was going to keep it secret, Molly. Superstition, I guess. Afraid it all might disappear. But it will be so good to talk about him with you."

Molly grinned widely, her blue eyes sparkling. "Him who? That's Question Number One."

"Him Hugh. That's who."

Molly flopped back, her mouth open, her eyes huge, and her brows climbing toward the ceiling. "Our Hugh? How on earth…? Last time I knew, you two were barely speaking."

"Well, he asked me to go somewhere with him. We decided on the outdoor museum." She could feel herself starting to blush. "And we spent the night together."

"Yay for the silent Scot!"

"He's not always that silent."

Molly's eyes widened in amused delight, and Ivy's face was immediately flooded with scarlet.

"No. I didn't mean—I meant he, we, we did a lot of talking."

Molly studied her friend's rosy face. "So it's not just lust."

"Well, there's a lot of lust. A wondrously huge amount of lust. I had no idea… But I like him too. I respect him." She straightened the container of paper clips on her desk. "And I think I'll like and respect him more and more as I get to know him better. He's a good man, Molly. He's interesting. Smart. Caring. Complicated."

"All characteristics that describe you too."

Ivy looked startled. "Oh. Thank you." She stood up. "This has been the most exciting thing in my whole life, Moll. I *loved* having sex with Hugh. But I also liked sleeping with him, actually sleeping. And talking. And eating breakfast."

"Better than your previous experiences?"

"No. I haven't had any bad experiences." She lifted her chin, her cheeks still red. "I haven't had any experiences. At all. I suppose I should be embarrassed to admit, even to you, that I was a virgin until yesterday. But I'm actually more glad than embarrassed because I lucked into a first experience that was," she fumbled for the right word, "astonishing. Thrilling. Joyful."

"Wow. No wonder you're all twitterpated. It sounds like you went from nothing to jackpot with no awkward steps in between."

"It does feel like winning the lottery. Yes."

Molly contemplated her friend. "Your first time might not have been so good if you'd lost your virginity back in high school."

"With a boy."

"Wearing humongous sneakers and a backwards baseball cap."

"And not taking them off for sex."

"Which would last only a minute."

Ivy looked at her friend from under her lashes. "How about lasting maybe an *hour*?"

Molly let out a long whistle. "I'm going to be looking at that lanky Scot with considerable respect from now on." She leaned back against the wall and hugged her knees. "So he's insatiable?"

"I think we both are. Insatiable. Of course, it's all new to me so maybe this is normal. And it's likely to level off after a while, the—um—lust." She grinned. "I'm just hoping that after a while doesn't happen anytime soon."

"Hmmm. It's been a long time since my Ed and I have felt insatiable. In fact," she looked alarmed, "I think it's been almost a month since we last made love." The tiny woman jumped to her feet. "May I head home early? I think it's time for me to get creative."

"Oh, my. Your Ed's not going to know what hit him."

"That is my plan exactly."

Chapter Twenty-Two

After many weeks of summer heat and summer sunshine, the Grace's Warbler stopped singing its sweet song. It no longer felt compelled to signal a mate, to see a little female flying toward him, to copulate, nest and share the duties of feeding young. Instead, with every day that passed, the bird felt a stronger need to leave the pines around the reservoir and find its winter home.

One night, when the first stars appeared in the deep blue sky and a thin crescent moon bathed the woods in pale silver, the little bird flew up into the open sky for the first time since spring. Wings beating strongly, it left the woods near the granite ledge. It headed northeast, continuing in the same direction as its long, long flight from Mexico.

At dawn on the first morning of its fall migration, the warbler landed in a boggy area with spruce, pine, fir, and water. Nothing was familiar, but there were caterpillars to eat. After many minutes, a much larger bird took a few steps on a thick branch below the warbler, a bird the warbler hadn't noticed. The big bird, a Spruce Grouse, was no threat, and eventually the warbler went back to feeding.

Later that day, three birders walked below the tree, hoping to see a Canada Jay or maybe a Black-backed Woodpecker. They never knew about the rarity right above their heads.

On a moonless night, the bird once again flew over a border between two countries. But this time there were no desperate people stumbling through the dark below, no armed border patrol agents trying to find them. Hour after hour, there was nothing below but trees.

Chapter Twenty-Three

When Ivy's little car rolled to a stop, Hugh was standing in the doorway, squinting into the evening sun, his feet bare and his thick hair damp and tousled.

"Hi."

"Hi." He bent and barely brushed her lips with his. "Come in."

She shrugged out of her backpack, set it on the low bench by the door, and handed him a quart of half-and-half.

"Thank you.... Come with me to the kitchen." He opened the fridge and spoke with his back to her. "You're probably tired. We should sit out on the patio. Let you relax."

"That sounds… okay. Thank you."

"Cheese and crackers."

"Okay."

"Also smoked trout paté." He opened a cupboard and got out a box of crackers.

"That sounds…" Frowning, Ivy looked at his back. "Hugh."

"What?"

"You're not meeting my eyes. At all." Ivy backed up a step and bumped into the island in the middle of the kitchen. "Are you regretting… this? Us? Do you want me to leave?"

"No!" He met her eyes then, his own startled and

earnest. "No! Not at all. I just..." A red stain spread across his cheekbones. "I was trying... I didn't want you to feel that I just want to... that I just want to rush you to bed."

"Oh. So you were thinking we should sit for a while in the kitchen..."

"On the patio. Actually. I was thinking we would sit out on the patio."

"On the patio, then. And we'd sip cocktails..."

He pointed toward two long-stemmed glasses and a corkscrew. "Wine."

"Okay. Wine." She bit her lip, her eyes beginning to laugh. "And we'd say things like How was your day, and... And nice weather, isn't it? And we'd be polite."

"Yes. Then we'd have a leisurely supper. With dessert. And maybe after-dinner cordials. And then..." He leaned back against the fridge, his eyes now warm and his face relaxed. "And then I was thinking we might sit for a while on the living room couch. Maybe do a little, uh, necking. Petting. And *then* we'd go to bed."

"Very civilized, Hugh."

"I thought so."

"But what if I want you to rush me off to bed?"

"Well then." He turned and carefully set the box of crackers on the counter. "Then I think I have an obligation, as host." He walked to her and put his hands on her upper arms. "The host should do what the guest wants."

She nodded. "It's only polite."

Hugh touched her mouth with his. They stood for many seconds, their lips touching, her hands lightly on his chest, his hands slowly moving up and down her arms.

"I need a shower, like yesterday. And your shower is just humongous. So on the ride over, I was thinking we should share."

"I just showered."

"One can never be too clean."

"Next to godliness?"

"Something like that."

He took her hand and led her out of the kitchen.

"Hugh?"

"Eh?"

"Why didn't we shower together yesterday?"

He shot her a look from under his brows. "I wanted us to make it into bed before I exploded."

"Oh."

They undressed quickly and Ivy felt a moment's astonishment that she didn't feel self-conscious.

"Hot enough?"

Her eyes widened.

"The water. Is this a good temperature?"

"Oh. Yes. The water's great."

He turned her with her back against his chest and his arms around her. She could feel his erection nudging her, and she watched him lathering his hands, turning the bar of soap over and over in his long fingers, cascades of bubbles falling to the tiled floor. She closed her eyes, almost ill with wanting. He soaped her neck, under her arms, around her breasts, lifting, smoothing, pulling her taut nipples. Then she felt his hands on her belly and then the insides of her thighs and then between her legs.

She sucked in a long shuddering breath. "Can we rush to bed right now?"

They were still dripping when they fell onto his quilt, their hands grasping, their mouths open and touching and tasting. When he came into her, she arched up and pulled him close with her hands and legs. After only seconds, she cried out and he started moving fast, his head lifted, his eyes fixed sightlessly at the wall. She strained up and felt him pumping deep inside.

Very slowly, he lowered his head and looked down at her, stunned brown eyes meeting stunned blue eyes.

"So," Ivy gasped. "Hugh. Hi. How was your day?"

She had never heard him laugh aloud before. Now his laugh filled the room, and she felt the deep rumble behind her breasts and low in her belly.

"Ivy. Sweet Ivy. The first part of my day and this last part were… they were exceptional." He bent and kissed her, breathless and still laughing. "The in-between part is pretty much a blur. Because I couldn't stop remembering the first part and anticipating this part."

"Me too." She reached up and touched his mouth with fingers that were still numb. "Wasn't this much better than trout paté?"

She felt his laughter inside her again.

"We probably should have toweled off. We got your bed sopping wet."

"I'll change the sheets in a few minutes. Are you chilly?"

"Not at all."

"Good. I'm not quite up to moving yet."

She tightened her inner muscles around his partially erect penis. "Hugh?"

"Mmm?"

"This is… weird."

The brown eyes were suddenly wary. "Weird? Why?"

"Just a few weeks ago, you were the, the new man

on the FATSO walks, the man who glared a lot and didn't say very much. And now…" She caressed his beard. "Now you're the man who's in bed with me." The corners of her mouth turned up. "The man whose body I can't stop wanting to touch. It feels, it seems like… It's a big change, Hugh. Like we took a giant step sideways into some other reality."

"A good reality."

"Oh god yes."

"I'm startled too, Ivy. I had good reason to believe that I would never be in bed with a woman again, ever."

"I'm glad that wasn't right. What you believed."

"As am I." His dark eyes were puzzled. "You like having me in you."

"I do."

"Tell me."

She traced the slight furrow between his brows. "I like having you in me, Hugh. I really like it."

"I am one lucky man." He moved a little. "Also very turned on. Which is ridiculous. I came about three minutes ago."

She felt him hardening again, lengthening.

"I might be in you for quite a while now."

"You mean we might be doing this for a long time? Ages?"

"That is what I mean. Yes."

"I am one lucky woman."

They moved together now as if they'd done it a thousand times before, watching each other, intent, slightly smiling.

"Put your legs down."

Ivy did as he asked and then was startled and dismayed when he pulled out of her.

"Hugh?"

"I wanted to do this yesterday." He moved down her body, kissing the inner slopes of her breasts and then her belly. "But I was afraid it might, you might…"

She felt his mouth against her damp curls.

"Ohhh god, Hugh."

When he parted her with his tongue, she grabbed two fistfuls of wet coverlet and arched into his mouth. This time when she came, tears came too, a breathless ecstatic rush of tears.

Hugh slid back up her body and into her again. She smelled her sex on his face, tasted herself on his tongue. He came again within seconds.

"Sorry," he panted. "I'm sorry, Ivy."

"These are happy tears."

"No. I mean… I thought I would last longer. You wanted me to last longer. Tasting you, your taste, having you in my mouth. Ivy. It tipped me over the edge."

She unclenched her fingers from his bottom and caressed his shoulders. "Don't apologize for the most… This was the most incredible thing in my whole life. Everything. Starting in the shower. Everything."

A corner of his mouth lifted. "All right then. I won't apologize." He slid out of her and rolled them over, draping her limp body over his, holding her close with one hand in her hair and the other splayed on her bottom. "That was the best ever for me too."

"Hugh?"

"Mmm?"

"I like sex."

"Yeah?"

"I really do. It's…" She kissed the side of his neck. "It's so much better than my very best fantasies."

"I'm glad."

"Hugh?"

"Mmm?"

"Is it going to keep on like this? Getting better and better?" She lifted her head and looked down at him, her eyes still starry with tears. "'Cause that's almost scary."

He laughed again, rocking her back and forth in his arms. Long moments passed in silence, until their breathing was almost back to normal.

"Hugh?"

"Mmm?"

"I'm hoping there's more for supper than paté."

"Salmon and corn on the cob, grilled. Orzo salad with vegetables and feta. Guido's tiramisu for dessert. Ready in about fifteen minutes."

"You are a truly wonderful person."

****

Hugh handed Ivy a wine glass for her to dry. "We have a few things to discuss about this coming week."

"Okay." She reached up and put the glass away, now at home in his kitchen. "But first, Hugh, I have to mention that you look extraordinarily sexy with your sleeves rolled up. You're usually so neat and collected. Sleeves rolled up or this wave that falls onto your forehead—They both make you look deliciously mussed up."

He caught her hand in his wet, sudsy one and placed a kiss on her wrist. "Turned on by a curl and a forearm." He twisted his mouth to hide a smile. "Saves a fortune on chocolate and red roses."

Ivy laughed with delight. "You almost never say anything flippant! Or tongue-in-cheek."

"Well, maybe…" He became still, his hands

motionless in the water. "Huh. I can't do it. I was trying to frame something witty. Something about all the time we've been spending tongue in cheek." He glanced at her sideways. "Tongues in each other's cheeks. Mouths." He shook his head ruefully. "But it was coming out more convoluted than silver-tongued."

"You don't need a silver tongue, Hugh." She hesitated, feeling her face get warm, and then she leaned close to his ear and whispered. "Your tongue is golden."

He cleared his throat. "Back to the topic at hand. This coming week."

"Okay. What do we have to discuss?"

"First, I never would have agreed to talk at this convention if it had come up after we became lovers, Ivy. I want you to know that." His dark eyes met hers. "Five days feels like a long time."

"Yes, it does. And five nights."

"Second," he handed her another wine glass, "While you were in the shower I switched my flight home from Sunday morning to the Saturday red-eye. I might be a bit bleary but I'm planning to show up for Sunday's FATSO walk."

Her face lit up. "So after birding we'll have the whole rest of Sunday to ourselves!"

He put his hands back in the sink and heaved a sigh. "I'll be exhausted, Ivy. I'll probably go right to sleep after we get back from the walk." He handed her a plate. "Unless you devise some scheme to keep me awake."

"I'll give it thought while you're gone."

A grin lifted one corner of his mouth. "So what's on for the FATSO group? Where are you taking us?"

"There's a drawdown in some of the impoundments at the wildlife center. We'll walk in about a half mile and set up scopes and hope to watch migrating shorebirds feasting on the yummy little invertebrates in the exposed mud." She put the plate in Hugh's cupboard and turned back to him. "This will be Jack's first time back after the accident so we needed a short walk on flat terrain, with lots of time to rest. He says he'll be fine as long as he doesn't carry anyone's scope and tripod."

Hugh handed her another plate.

"Shorebirding is really different from looking at songbirds, Hugh. If the birds find a good mud flat, they stay put for hours and hours. Even days. They don't even mind people close to them." She put the plate in the cupboard and then leaned toward him and kissed his jaw. "You said a few things."

"Hmm?"

"You said we have a few things to discuss. That's two, the convention and your flight. Is there something else on your mind?"

"Yes. I suggest that you stay here, Ivy, while I'm gone. In fact, I suggest that you move in."

"Oh." She backed up. "That feels... It would be odd to be here without you, Hugh. This is your house."

"And it's been my house for years, Ivy. But for the past few weeks, I've found myself thinking 'our bedroom'." He turned to face her squarely. "Why not our house?"

Ivy looked down at the dishtowel in her hand. "Your dish towels have birds on them."

"Irrelevant. But yes. They do."

"American Avocets."

"And Stilts. Black-necked Stilts, to be precise. Again, however, not relevant."

"They're both shorebirds. There's almost no chance

185

that we'll see these species next Sunday." She took a pie pan from the rack and stared down as she dried it. "And there are grouse on this pan. You've been a birder all along."

"I told you right from the start that I was interested in birds."

"True. And lucky, too. Or we might never have met each other."

"I would rather not think about that."

"I've never seen an avocet or a stilt."

"Me neither. Are you ready to go back to the topic at hand?"

"Moving in."

"Yes."

"That's a… That's a very big step."

"You've been here every night for three weeks. Every breakfast and every supper. Your toothbrush and hairbrush and deodorant and shampoo are here."

"But we're still… Hugh, we're new lovers still. I'm ignorant about… I'm not up on, I don't know what people usually do but…"

"I'm not talking about what people usually do. I'm talking about you and me. We two have taken every step in this relationship in our own unique order."

Her lips curved up. "That's true."

"And you said your apartment is tiny and, I think you said, uninteresting. What ties you to it?"

"Nothing, Hugh. I'm not tied to it. But…"

"And you have said that you like my house."

"I love it. It's beautiful, and gracious, and welcoming."

"You said you feel at home here."

"I do. But…" She looked out the window, gathering

her thoughts. "Moving in together is a big step. We're, I think we're both sex-drunk, Hugh. People who are drunk, on *anything*, shouldn't be making serious decisions."

"Sex drunk."

"Yes. At least I am. I can't think of anything but sex. It's astonishing." She studied his face, her eyes serious. "I'm… We're both still taken with the newness of it all. I was a virgin. And you were…"

"A eunuch."

Ivy blinked. "I was going to say celibate. But okay. A virgin and a eunuch who have just discovered sex together. That doesn't seem like a good pair to be making big decisions." She smoothed his beard with her fingers. "Hugh, this is my first experience with something that's so much more exciting and wonderful than I'd ever dreamed. My first sex. My first man."

"Interesting choice of words." He turned away from her and carefully rinsed a salad bowl. "Have you been thinking ahead to your second man?"

"Nope. I have no interest in sex with anyone but you." She took the bowl from his hand and put it away. When she turned back, Hugh was staring down at the water in the sink, his shoulders stiff and his eyes bleak.

"My god! You *meant* that question!"

"You said it, Ivy. You can't think of anything but sex. It would be natural for you to want to experience it with a, a somewhat broader sample of the male population."

Ivy put the dishtowel on the counter. "You listen to me. Yes, I think about sex all the time now, and it's always you. I am besotted with you. I'm amazed at how much and how often I want to have sex with you. There is absolutely no room left for even random thoughts about anyone else."

He didn't move.

"Do you hear me?"

"Yes."

"Do you believe me?"

His shoulders relaxed a little. "Of course I do, Ivy. Everything you do tells me that you've been happy with me since we became lovers. My question was out of line. And idiotic."

"It was."

He glanced at her from the corner of his eye. "I believe you. But I'm having trouble believing *this*. How life has been recently."

Ivy put her arms around him from the back and hugged him hard. "Me too."

"Really?"

"I find myself making up reasons why I deserve all this. Deserve you. Like, I gave up a happy and contented life at the commune to care for my mother. And I've helped a lot of people enjoy nature." She kissed the smooth cotton covering his spine. "I can make sense of this only if you're some sort of karmic reward."

Hugh pulled her closer, rubbing his hands along her arms. "You know, Ivy, there are people who could just accept this as something they confidently expect from life. It appears that neither of us is in that privileged group."

Ivy rubbed her cheek against his shoulder. "Is that why you suggested moving in? Would it make you more sure about us?"

He caressed her hands, tickling the sensitive places between her fingers. "I hadn't thought of it that clearly.

But yes. Having you here when I'm gone would, I don't know…"

"Ensure that I'm here when you get back."

"Yes."

"I'm not ready to move in, Hugh."

"I was wrong to pressure you."

"No. You weren't wrong. You were honest."

"And you're honestly not ready."

"No." She pushed his loose collar aside with her chin and kissed his neck. "But I will sleep here one or two nights this week. In your bed."

"Our bed."

"Okay. Our bed."

"I will love thinking that you might be here."

They stood in silence, feeling each other's warmth.

"There's one more thing, Ivy. To discuss."

"Yes?"

"And it's big."

"Oh dear."

"Sunday will be the first FATSO walk since we became lovers." Hugh went on before she could answer. "And don't say we should keep it a secret. Every time I get near you, your face gets rosy." He dropped a kiss on her mouth. "I find that amazing, by the way. That your face gets pink when I come within a few yards of you. And then I start drooling."

"You do not drool."

"All right. I don't drool. Visibly. But anybody who sees me with you would know we're lovers."

"You haven't been looking all severe and disapproving, that's for sure. Like you did the first many times I saw you."

"I imagine I look stunned. And incessantly horny."

"Horny is a good look for you. Horny and sexy and gorgeous." She put her hands on his wrists and slid them under his rolled-up sleeves. "Anyway, I wasn't going to say we should keep us a secret. I was going to suggest…" She looked thoughtful. "Okay. Here's what I suggest. We wait for the ideal moment on the walk, when every single birder is looking in our direction, and then I walk up to you, lean in close, kiss you on the mouth and rub my boobs against your chest."

"That could work."

"And I'd grab your butt at the same time."

"Complex move."

"Very."

"I think it would behoove us to practice."

"Behoove, huh? I don't think I've ever behooved in my life. I know I've never participated in mutual behoovement. Behooverry."

"I think we'll both like it."

Chapter Twenty-Four

As night fell, the Grace's Warbler flew through a black and silver world. Under a moonless sky pricked by tiny silver stars. Over velvet black forests of spruce and balsam. Over countless lakes, ponds, rivers, and streams gleaming like bands and pools of mercury. Other migrants were in the air, all heading in the opposite direction. Twice that night, the vagrant faltered and half-turned. But each time it returned to its northeast path, the futile path that was taking it farther and farther from where it belonged.

Over eastern Quebec, the Grace's Warbler flew into the remnants of an Atlantic hurricane. Pushed fast and hard by the wind, the little bird struggled to land. But there was nothing below but fog and ocean, and no way to turn back.

Chapter Twenty-Five

"Jack! It is a true delight to see you here! And upright!"

His broad face was thinner than before, but he shot out of the back seat of Molly's car, talking before both feet were on the ground, looking all around and beaming. "Yes, yes, Ivy! It IS a true delight to be here! I am telling you all, as a solemn oath, that I intend never to do that near-death thing again."

Ivy laughed and kissed his cheek. "A very good decision, Jack."

"Hug everybody! Gotta! I'm alive and well and I gotta hug everyone!" Grinning widely, Jack gave quick bear hugs to Charlie, Molly, and Sean. "Beck and Josef coming? And Hugh?"

"I think so. Beck knows where to find us."

"All RIGHT! Lead on, fearless and all-knowing leader! Oh wait! My cane!"

He reached into the back of Molly's car and pulled out a bright orange cane carved to look like a flamingo.

"Ta Da!"

"That is truly magnificent, Jack! Perfect for a birder!"

"A gift from dear friends." He brandished the cane like a sword in front of him. "Now you can lead on!"

The day was cool for August, with fast-moving gray and white clouds and only occasional appearances of the warming sun. The group walked first through woods along a dirt road wide enough for regular monitoring trips by Fish and Wildlife vehicles. When they reached the first of several earthen embankments, Ivy stopped.

"We'll bushwhack off to the left here. Sometimes there are good mudflats just beyond that line of trees." She looked back down the trail. "Hugh's going to be late. He won't know where we're going, so he's likely to keep walking on the main trail. I'll wait here and catch him. Sean, take my scope so you guys can get started ogling shorebirds without me."

"See you in a little while." Molly winked, and Ivy felt herself flush.

Canada Geese honked from the water. A dapper Eastern Kingbird squeaked from the top of a willow. Blue-green Tree Swallows swooped over the field. A male bluebird stood on top of a nesting box, ready to defend his mate and their second clutch of young if any of the swallows happened to mistake his box for theirs.

Ivy tilted her head up into a wide band of sunlight streaming down between two gray-edged clouds. Finally she saw Hugh's tall form coming out of the woods, his eyes on the ground in front of him, his face set and stern. She started walking to meet him and felt a rush of delight when he looked up and she saw his slow smile.

"Hi."

"Hi."

"Where is everybody?"

"They're up there, to the left."

He touched her cheek. "This is ridiculous. It feels like it's been weeks and weeks since I've seen you."

"Me too." Ivy smoothed her hands over the front of his flannel shirt. "I've slept alone my whole life but these last few nights felt wrong."

"Thank you for leaving the message that you were sleeping in my bed." He briefly looked fierce. "*Our* bed. It meant a lot to me."

"I'm glad." Ivy slid her arm around his waist and he pulled her closer, his long fingers caressing her hip.

"I wanted to call you back that night but it was after midnight your time."

"Carousing?"

"Seminar."

"Seminar till the wee hours. Sounds like carousing to me."

"Alas. It was truly a seminar—and an unexpectedly lengthy and contentious one."

"Contentious architects? You guys who use bricks and wood are morons! Concrete rules!"

She could feel his silent chuckle.

"The topic was bird-friendly skyscrapers. You know, ways to prevent birds from crashing into them and being killed." He kissed her dark curls. "I hadn't realized that the numbers are so astronomical. Maybe as many as a billion birds a year, world-wide, die from crashing into windows."

"Yikes. That's very depressing."

"Worse, some people don't even think it's a real problem. One guy pointed at a row of pigeons on a nearby roof and said, 'See? There are lots of birds'."

"Oh, dear." She sighed and leaned her head against his shoulder.

"The American Institute of Architects has had a bird-friendly building committee for several years. As of a few days ago, I'm on it."

Ivy stopped walking and turned to him. "That's

wonderful, Hugh. You'll be such a good advocate!"

She wrapped her arms around him and leaned into his wonderfully familiar touch and taste.

After many seconds, she took a deep breath. "Well. Yes. That should do it."

Hugh raised his eyebrows. "It doesn't do it for me. Not even close."

"I mean it'll do for letting the others know about us." She jerked her head to one side, and Hugh looked up. The rest of the group was just coming into view where the side trail branched off from the dirt road.

"How did you know they were coming?"

"The tripods clank."

He nuzzled her neck. "Good ears."

"Birder's ears."

"Well. In for a penny, in for a pound."

"Pardon?"

"British saying." He spoke his next words against her mouth. "It means, why do something halfway?"

The next time Ivy leaned back in his arms, her eyes were slightly unfocused. "Are you pleased with yourself?"

"Eh?"

"You have turned me into a breathless and boneless puddle of desire."

She was laughing as she turned to face the group of birders. At the head of the line, Jack had stopped dead, his face a mask of astonished delight.

Ivy raised her voice. "You guys gave up awfully quickly. Nothing interesting?"

"Nothing interesting 'til right now! Jeez, a guy spends a few days in a coma and misses all sorts of stuff." He turned to the others. "Why didn't anybody tell me about this development?"

"It hasn't been public knowledge until today." Molly tucked her arm under his. "This is the first time any of us have seen the silent Scot in courtship plumage. Observe the heightened color in the face and neck. The added brightness in the eyes. The mussed-up hair, reminiscent of the erected crowns of male titmice, cardinals, and kinglets."

Hugh tightened his hands on Ivy's shoulders and she tilted her head to rub her cheek against his fingers.

"Pair bonding behaviors." Jack's bright eyes went back and forth between the lovers. "Once again, a FATSO trip rewards us with the unexpected!"

Ivy looked at Charlie. "Are there any shorebirds?"

"Nothing down here. We were gonna head down to the end of the trail. More exposed mud."

"Hold on a minute. Here comes Beck."

The woman was hastening along the path, bent over an awkward pile of something in her arms.

"I am sorry. I am late, I know. I had… I had unexpected difficulty this morning. And then I could not determine how to get the scope on the tripod. Josef always does that."

Charlie reached out, took the scope from Beck's arms, and handed it to Hugh. Then he took the tripod, extended the legs, and set it on the ground.

"Thought so. One of those kinds." He took the scope again. "Here. Now you can carry the whole shebang."

"Thank you." Beck hoisted the tripod and scope over her shoulder.

"Should we wait here for Josef?"

"Josef is not coming. Josef is gone."

In silence, the group watched her long form stalk

down the trail away from them.

"What do you think?" Molly murmured. "Did she knock him out with his giant lens and bury him in the pile of manure from those blasted chickens?"

****

At first glance, the mudflats appeared empty. Brown mud and tan mud and grayish dried mud, puddles of glistening muddy water, old mud-covered lily pads flopping up and down in the breeze, the pointed leaves and dying purple flowers of pickerel weed.

"There's nothing here." Sean's young voice cracked twice in the short sentence.

"Don't give up so fast. Look through your binocs. Scan slowly. Look for small movements or rounded shapes."

"Oh! I was wrong! There's... Wow!"

Scores of little birds were walking around on the mud, their cryptic coloring making them almost invisible at first glance. More small shapes huddled motionless, each behind its own little root or bit of tree trunk.

"This is so weird! It's like there was nothing there and then they all just came right up out of the mud!"

"Get out those guidebooks and get ready for some serious ID work, friends!" Jack was bouncing with excitement. "We Vermonters only get a few days a year to study shorebirds!"

For the next hour, the shorebirds fed and the humans watched. Finally, Jack made a snorting sound and lowered his binoculars. "I've about had it. I've got the yellowlegs and the plovers of course, and I think I'm set with the semipalms and leasts. But a possible-but-not-likely White-rumped Sandpiper? That's stretching my brain."

Hugh nodded. "Me too."

Beck was standing behind her scope, staring out across the mudflats. "The chickens."

"Pardon?"

"He killed the chickens." She turned to the others, her eyes puzzled and pained. "Josef killed all of the chickens. Every single one. Before he left. I kicked him out so he killed the chickens."

"Oh, Beck!"

"He didn't just kill them, out in the coop. He put them around the house for me to find. A dead Barred Rock hen in the kitchen, in my chair. A Buff Orpington on the counter. With its head in the butter dish."

Beck was shivering.

"On the porch. On… It doesn't matter. We're here to watch shorebirds."

Charlie took off his flannel shirt and draped it over Beck's shoulders.

"What did you do with the chickens?"

"Nothing. I didn't do anything with them yet. They've been there since last night. So they're wasted. No more…" She gulped. "No more cacciatore. They're just garbage."

It was a subdued group as they left the mudflats. Ivy dropped back, letting most of the group get several yards ahead. Next to her, Hugh spoke very quietly. "Charlie said he's going to stay with Beck tonight."

"That's a good idea."

"I suggested that I could stay too."

"Oh?"

"He said, and I quote, you've got a woman achin' to be alone with you." He put his arm around her shoulders. "Is that true? Are you achin'?"

"I am. It's true." Ivy leaned into his solid warmth. "And I'm grateful for having something to think about other than Beck and Josef… and the chickens."

"Me too."

She slid her arm around his waist. "It must be quite a burden, Hugh."

"Eh?"

"Your sudden fame as a stud muffin. They all can see that you turn me to goo."

"FYI, Ivy." His long fingers slid over her shoulder until he could touch the top of her breast. "You forgot my butt."

"Beg pardon?"

"You said you were going to grab my butt. When we let the others know about us."

"Oh." She slid her hand down from his waist.

From behind them Jack called out, "Keep it decent up there, you two! Man in a weakened state back here."

Ivy laughed as she and Hugh stopped and turned. "Sorry, Jack. I forgot all about you. How are you holding up?"

Jack's eyes were sparkling but his round face was paler than usual and he was sweating heavily. "My legs have a tendency to go all jelly-like without warning." He looked past Ivy and nodded. "I think I'll just sit for a minute." He gingerly lowered himself onto a convenient rock. "I've been talking to them sternly. My legs. They've agreed to support me a while longer."

"Have you had any water today?"

Jack tilted sideways and dug into a pocket on the side of his pants leg.

"This." He held up a small flask. "I didn't bring anything bigger because I didn't want the weight."

"For Pete's sake, Jack! Why didn't you say something? Here." Ivy took an almost full bottle from one of the mesh pockets of her vest.

"Thanks. That'll help." He took a long drink and then looked up, his eyes mischievous. "Now if anyone happens to have any dark chocolate…"

Hugh silently handed him a bag of chocolate-covered almonds.

"Miraculous. Fat, sugar, caffeine, and protein. Some more water and a couple of these and I'll be right as rain."

They all watched as Jack slowly ate several nuts and then held the bag out. "Take them, Hugh. As my old daddy used to say, I may not have had enough but I have had a sufficiency." He put both hands on the rock and pushed himself upright. "I'm ready. Let's go."

Ivy watched Jack take a few uneven steps and then settle into a regular walking rhythm.

"Wait, Hugh. Let's bring up the rear." With no one in back of them anymore, she slipped her hand into the back pocket of his jeans. "You didn't have a great first experience with shorebirding, Hugh. Want to come back next Sunday?

"The birds will still be around?"

"Probably. Unless Fish and Wildlife raises the water level. There might be different species, too."

"Goody. A greater variety of identical tan blobs."

"Well, Charlie's planning a trip up to the ledge." She smiled at him. "Our ledge. With Sean's afterschool nature club. Five or six junior high kids. We could go with them instead."

"Let's come back here."

"Good. I'd like that too."

"Has anyone seen the warbler recently?"

"Not for a few weeks. Charlie wants to see if it's spending all its time up away from the parking lot and the logging road."

"It could have left the area entirely."

"True."

"Or been caught by a hawk."

"Also true."

After a few more minutes, she felt and heard him chuckle. "What?"

"I was just reviewing some words and phrases from today."

"Semipalmated? White-rumped?"

"Nope." His white smile flashed briefly. "Stud muffin. Goo. Puddle of desire. To answer your question of a few hours back, yes, Ivy. I am inordinately pleased with myself. And you. And life."

Under her fingers, Ivy felt a change in the flex and movement of his muscles.

"You're strutting."

"A little, yes."

They reached the cars just as Charlie was saying, "Molly, you've got to get Jack home."

"Yup. Nap time. Rose'll call out the National Guard if I'm late."

"Sean, you go with them. Or your mom'll be calling the Guard too." Charlie turned to Beck. "The rest of us are following you home. Make sure the house is empty."

"Why? Of course not. I'll be fine."

"Not up for discussion."

Ivy nodded. "We have to know you're safe, Beck."

"On the way, we can stop at a hardware store and buy a few deadbolts so we can change the locks." Hugh looked at Charlie. "You've got a tool kit in your car, right?"

Beck's head snapped up. "I have tools. I was a homeowner alone for years."

"Sorry. I didn't mean to be patronizing. We'll use your tools to change the locks, and then we'll deal with the chickens."

"And then I'm staying."

Beck turned toward Charlie with a fierce scowl, but Ivy reached out and touched her arm.

"Charlie's being sensible, Beck. He should stay."

"Josef is long gone. He is not a threat."

"Hurting animals is a danger sign, Beck." Molly was uncharacteristically somber. "It's often a precursor, a sign that there's potential there for hurting humans. And enjoying it."

"He didn't hurt the chickens. He wrung their necks, just like I did with the one I cooked."

"But leaving them around like that is not normal. And it's creepy."

Beck looked around at them all. "All right. Stay tonight, Charlie. Maybe I can get some sleep if you're there." Her eyes stopped at Ivy and Hugh, who were standing with their arms around each other.

"I've missed something. What's up with those two?"

"They're in a relationship, Beck." Molly's eyes sparkled as she watched Hugh drop a kiss on Ivy's mouth. "It was the big surprise of the morning. Even better than the White-rumped Sandpiper."

"I should… I should be happy for them. But I'm not. I'm anxious for her."

Charlie growled. "Hugh is a good man."

"A very good man," Ivy added.

"And Josef isn't."

"No."

"You all knew that."

"Yes."

Beck looked again at Hugh and Ivy, watching them in silence for a long moment. "Josef would be making a joke. Mocking. If he were here." Then, an eerie imitation of Josef's rich baritone. "So! *Somebody* here knows what that Scotsman has under his kilt!"

Chapter Twenty-Six

Ivy brought her little Fiat to a stop. The parking lot was full and cars lined both sides of the dirt road leading to the trails.

"Drat. I forgot about the godwit."

"Eh?"

"It was on the birders' listserv. A guy from Middlebury thought he might have seen a Black-tailed Godwit here yesterday evening."

"That would be a rarity?"

"Big one! A Black-tailed Godwit has been seen in Vermont only once. Maybe twice."

"Large shorebirds. Right?"

"Yes. With long legs and long blunt two-toned bills that turn up very slightly." She edged the car between two SUVs, then made a u-turn in the back parking lot and parked under an oak with wide branches. "It's cloudy today but I still go for the shade. Force of habit."

They reached into the car's tiny back seat and gathered their equipment.

"I'm sorry I didn't think about the godwit, Hugh. I figured most birders have already had a full week to study whatever's feeding on the mud flats so we might have the place and the shorebirds to ourselves. But it's a weekend and it's not pouring…" She eyed the gray sky. "Yet." She wiggled into her binocular harness. "And now with the possibility of a rarity, we're going to have a crowd."

"It'll still be just the two of us birding. We can interact with other people or not, whatever we feel like at the moment."

"That's true." She reached into one of her vest pockets and took out a green plastic bottle. "With yesterday's rain and today's humidity, the walk through the woods is going to be a mosquito frenzy. Want some?"

"They don't usually bother me."

She sprayed some bug repellant on her hand and then rubbed it on her neck and ears and elbows. "Lucky you. The critters just love nibbling on me."

"As do I."

Her eyes widened. "It always startles me when you do that."

"Nibble?"

"No. You usually look so somber and self-contained and formal. Then suddenly your face changes." She flushed. "You turn into the person you are in bed. It completely knocks me off my feet."

His mouth softened in one of his rare slow smiles. "Good."

"It is. It's very good." She reached up but caught herself before her fingers touched his mouth. "Ick. Bug dope." She leaned in and kissed him instead. "There. My lips aren't icky."

"Never."

They walked along a broad embankment with water on both sides, the air full of the smells of rotting vegetation and damp dust.

"Black-tailed Godwit, huh?"

"Yes. Limosa limosa."

"Good god, Ivy. Do you know the scientific names of every bird you see?"

"Heavens no. Very few, actually. Turdus migratorius for robin. Mostly because it cracks up younger birders. The turdus part. Oh! And how about this one? Histrionicus histrionicus."

"Let me guess. It's something noisy. Crazy sounding. A loon?"

"Good guess—but no, it's Harlequin Ducks, little sea ducks that look they were designed by Dr. Seuss in collaboration with that female painter. Joan Miro, I think I mean. Apparently they're very noisy little critters."

"Miro was a man."

"Really? Named Joan."

"Really. Catalan, I think."

"I was right about the mosquitos." Ivy swatted the air with her free hand. "Did you have to take art courses as part of your architecture major?"

"They weren't required but I took several. Where can they be found?"

"Pardon?"

"Harlequin Ducks."

"Oh. In the winter they're off the coast of Massachusetts or Maine. I always say I'm going to take a trip but I never have."

"This coming winter, then. We'll ask Molly to cover for you so we can take a few days and find us a few examples of Histrionicus histrionicus."

"Ah. Open air again. Your walking smorgasbord is leaving, you foul flying fiends."

The little bluff above the mudflats was crowded with birders from all over the state. As they reached the top of the trail, Ivy called out, "Jack! You look very comfy! The chair is a stylish addition."

"Taking my birding easy!" He grinned at them both and gestured toward a small cooler at his feet. "Even got a sandwich and a cold drink."

"Elegant. But toting all that gear can't have been easy."

"Rose, my dear wonderful pregnant nonbirding Rose, walked in with me, got me set up, and is going to come back for me in, let's see. In two and a half hours." He winked at Hugh. "I'm telling you, Hugh. A loving woman is worth double her weight in gold. No! Triple!"

Ivy turned toward the mud flats. "Any godwit sightings?"

"Nope. No joy in Mudville for godwit hunters. Or I should say, Mudflat-ville. But for birders like you who like whatever birds show up, there's a lot to enjoy."

Hugh panned the scope across the mudflats and made a sound deep in his throat. "More variety than last week, I think."

"Excellent. Are you ready for some serious shorebird learning?"

"All right, instructor. Instruct." The corner of his mouth twitched. "I'm all yours."

She flushed. "Well, the yellowlegs are still here. Both kinds. And lots of peeps, including Least Sandpipers, Semipalmated Plovers, and Semipalmated Sandpipers. And there are a few Killdeer. Plus a Wilson's Snipe!"

"That chubby little striped guy?"

"Yes, exactly!"

"What's it doing?"

Ivy giggled. "I love that. Snipe and woodcocks do that. Woodcocks even more. They stand in one place and bounce up and down. Like a little dance."

"Why?"

"Best guess is that it agitates living things that are under the mud. Worms."

Jack lifted his soda can from the chair's cup holder. "Or it could be dancing. Just dancing. Humans aren't the only ones who can feel happy."

****

Hugh raised his arms over his head and stretched. "I've about had it. My muscles are tired, my brain is overflowing, and my stomach is getting empty. And it's starting to drizzle."

"Me, too." Ivy turned to Jack. "Rose should be here any minute. Want to walk with us toward the cars? We can carry your stuff."

"No. I'll wait for her. I want to show her some shorebirds." He grinned. "I keep hoping that eventually one bird will grab her. Seduce her into birding."

As they started down the slope, other birders were just arriving. One called up, "Is it here?"

"Is what here?"

"The Black-tailed Godwit!"

"Oh. No. No one's seen it today. Almost a dozen other shorebird species though."

The approaching trio stopped dead in the trail. "Crap. Might as well leave." They did an about-face and headed back down the slope.

"I just don't get it, Hugh. Look at them. Not one of them is smiling. All of their faces are set on grouch, grouch, grouch." Ivy shook her head. "Because they didn't find the 'good bird'. Lots of birds here, great birds, interesting birds. But they don't count."

"Because they're not rare."

"Because other people have seen them. As if a bird's intrinsic worth depreciates every single time another person sets eyes on it."

"But you understand why rarities are exciting."

"I do. Of course. It was incredibly exciting to see the Grace's Warbler. I wanted to see it again and again. But I don't understand why all the other birds are worthless. Why birders don't just enjoy birding!"

She made a wide gesture with her hands. "Look around. We're in this beautiful spot. It's sprinkling, sure, but it's a nice warm rain. We're feeling a gentle breeze on our skin. We live in a part of the world where big tracts of land like this have been set aside just so people can get out and enjoy nature. And not just rich people! Plus we're in a country where there hasn't been war for generations. We can go birding without even a passing thought to land mines or snipers or bombs from the sky. That's not the case in huge areas of the world." She gulped. "And all of those people are in good enough health to be walking. And they have access to transportation, to get out to this beautiful preserve. And they obviously have free time, time for hobbies and pastimes, time that doesn't have to be spent worrying about merely surviving. That's not the norm for humans throughout history, Hugh, or for humans across the globe even today."

"I love you."

Ivy froze.

Hugh stood looking at her, frowning slightly, his eyes intent.

When Ivy broke the silence, her voice was rough and whispery. "That's a somewhat drastic way of getting me to shut up. You could have just said 'Ivy, get off your soap box'."

"I didn't want to tell you to get off your soap box. I wanted to tell you that I love you."

Ivy stared at him for several more seconds and then made an abrupt movement and looked up at the sky. "I don't want my scope to get soaked. Let's go."

"Why are you angry?"

"I'm not angry."

"She says, with a fierce scowl."

"I am not angry. But I don't want to talk about this right now."

"Ivy! Hugh! I'm so glad to see you!"

Jack's wife Rose was puffing up the slope toward them, her arms cradling her swollen belly and her gentle features tight with worry. "The car was making funny noises, hiccupping or something, and then it totally died, just as I got here. Triple A's coming and I want to go back to the parking lot and wait for them but Jack shouldn't have to wait. He needs to get home and lie down for a while. Will you help me get his stuff and then give him a ride home?"

Ivy rearranged her features into something like a smile. "Of course, Rose. No trouble."

****

"I'm going to drop you off first, Hugh. Then I'll take Jack home and then I've got to, uh, I need to do something at the shop. I'll call you later today."

He didn't answer. Jack was dozing in the back seat, and there was silence in the car, the same uncomfortable silence that had surrounded them the whole ride home.

When Ivy pulled to a stop in front of Hugh's house, he looked at her wordlessly, got out of the car, and closed the door with exaggerated care.

****

Safe in the back room of her shop, Ivy took off her shoes, unlocked the metal cabinet and hung her wet birding vest on the corner of the door. She pulled off her equally wet t-shirt, dropped it on the floor, dragged one of the big plastic boxes from under the bed and pushed the lid to one side.

"Ivy, open the door."

She didn't answer, didn't move.

"Ivy. I just saw you go in there. Open the door."

She threw the door open. "*What*."

Hugh stepped in. His eyes took in the daybed and the box of clothes and the open locker. "Now there are two things to talk about. First. Do you live here?"

"What of it?"

"Does anyone know you're living here?"

"Of course not. Don't be idiotic. No one's supposed to live here."

"You could have told me."

She picked up a dry t-shirt from the box and pulled it on over her wet bra. "And how was I supposed to do that? Meet you and say 'hi, I'm Ivy, I'm illicitly living in the mall'? It was none of your business."

"And it's still none of my business?"

She sat down on the edge of the daybed, her spine straight, staring at his shirt buttons, not meeting his eyes. "I was going to tell you. I should have told you. I kept thinking of ways to tell you." She swallowed. "But I didn't want you to think I'm odd. Or eccentric."

"I do think you're odd and eccentric. And I do love you. And I want you to tell me why you find that so unwelcome."

She stared at the floor. The silence stretched. Hugh

waited.

Finally Ivy raised her head. "You knew I was in a bad mood! I told you!"

His eyes widened in disbelief. "You were in a bad mood."

"Yes! Those awful birders who didn't want to look at sandpipers. And the mosquitos!"

"You didn't want to hear that I love you because of mosquitoes? Are you listening to yourself at all?"

"I'm listening to *you*! You're yelling! And part of me wants to yell right back. Yell and yell and yell and then make you leave. I'm so angry at you for taking my attention away from what we have right now!" Her eyes filled with tears. "I am so happy with you, Hugh. I lo… I like every single minute we're together. Why can't you just be happy with that? Why can't you just let us go on day after day, being deliriously happy, just the way we are? Why do you have to bring love into it?" She lifted her chin and glared at him. "And how do you know you love me?"

"That's a ridiculous question."

"Maybe it's just sex. Elaine didn't like sex and that made you unhappy. And hurt your, your self-esteem. I like sex with you. That's got to make you, uh, ebullient."

"Ebullient."

"That's a real word!"

"I know it is."

"So maybe you just think you love me. Because you're feeling good. And happy."

Hugh clenched his hands at his sides. "And maybe you have it completely backwards, Ivy. Maybe sex is so good for us because we love each other."

There was a long pause. When he continued, his

voice was gentler. "Admitting that we love each other should make things better, Ivy. Not—"

She interrupted him, her voice loud and her face distorted. "Jack almost died."

"What?"

"A dumpster fell on him from out of the blue and then a tiny germ or virus or something almost killed him. A stupid absolutely unpredictable once-in-forever accident, and he almost ended up dead. His wife almost had to raise their baby alone."

Hugh took two steps away from the door, reached out a long arm, and grabbed the back of Ivy's desk chair. He wheeled it close to the daybed and sat down. "He didn't die. However, I get your point."

"I haven't reached my point yet."

"Loving someone means risk. Accidents happen. People get life-threatening infections. Or illness. Sometimes they die."

She glared at him. "And you're almost two years older than I am. Men die younger anyway."

Hugh made a helpless gesture with one hand, but she kept talking.

"When you told me about your dog, I said you were lucky to have had him and you said maybe you weren't. Weren't lucky. Because you got to love him and then he died. Well, I don't want to love you and then, and then have you die in another house fire, or have a car accident, or get cancer, or have a heart attack." Her voice broke. "And die."

"Ivy, I—"

"And look at Beck and Josef. They lived together. They probably slept together. They bought chickens together! And now she hates him. Hates! And he killed

213

the chickens."

"Do you think I'm going to turn into a, a Josef?"

"Of course not."

"Well?"

"But Beck might have thought he was a good person, when they started out…" She shrank back against the wall. "I have almost no experience with love. Love is something other people do. Not me."

"That's ridiculous."

"It's not! I don't even know what it looks like. My parents had a loveless marriage. And they didn't feel a whole lot of love for me."

"How do you know that?"

She met his eyes, her chin up. "My mother told me."

"In so many words? Ivy, we never loved you?"

"Yes! Pretty much. She said she would have left my father if she hadn't become pregnant. She said I was like a door with a huge padlock on it, slamming closed between her and the life she could have… Could have had without me."

"Ivy, that's terrible."

"It's not. Not completely. Not totally. I got to know Christine, my mother, my Christine, when she was in the nursing home. She got to know me." She twisted her hands together. "I think she loved me, then."

"I'm sorry, Ivy."

There was quiet around them. Outside, a police car went by, its siren wailing.

"What about the other part?

"What?"

"You said part of you wants to yell at me and kick me out. What does the other part want?"

Ivy stared at him for a long moment, her body stiff

and tense. Then she slumped. "The rest of me wants to admit that I love you too." She gazed at him helplessly, her eyes swimming in tears. "The rest of me wants to say I love you over and over until I've said it to every square inch of you."

"Let's go with that part." He got out of the chair, pushed it toward Ivy's desk, and shoved the box of clothes under the bed with his foot. Then he tossed the bolsters off the daybed, sat down and bent to untie his shoes.

"What are you doing?"

"I'm preparing for you to say I love you to every square inch."

"This bed is very narrow."

"We'll manage."

"This will be different, Hugh."

He paused with one shoe off and looked up at her.

"This will be the first time after we both said I love you."

"We haven't. Technically. You only said you'd like to say it."

"I love you."

He bent to take off his other shoe.

"Hugh. I love you."

He looked up then, his dark eyes gentle. "I'm very glad." He stood and unfastened his belt.

"This is going to be different," she repeated. "I feel like I'm going to start crying when you come into me."

"You're already crying."

"No. I mean sobbing. Maybe I'll be sobbing the whole time."

"That will be all right, Ivy."

Ivy stood watching him unbutton his shirt. Then she took a step toward him. "Okay then."

Chapter Twenty-Seven

Ivy put her shaking hand on the phone.

"Idiotic. Absurd. I love him. I even say it now. He loves me, and he says it all the time. Why can't I ask him a simple question without falling apart?"

She jumped when he answered.

"Hugh? May I… May I come over after work?"

There was silence. Then he spoke slowly and cautiously. "I thought that was a given."

"Oh. Yes. It is. Of course. But I mean… May I bring boxes with me when I come tonight? Clothes and things?"

There was an even longer pause.

"Oh. Maybe you've changed your mind. You said… A few weeks ago. You said I should move in. And I've been thinking about it. And I thought… But maybe you've changed your mind."

Now his voice was warm and husky. "Bring over boxes. Yes. Everything. That would be good, Ivy."

****

"I can easily move my clothes around and make room for yours. But it probably makes more sense to go out and get you a dresser of your own."

"Oh! I have one!" She turned and stared at him, her eyes huge. "I forgot all about the furniture!"

"The furniture?"

"In the barn. After my dad died, I put a few things

in his neighbor's barn. I completely forgot!"

"There's a dresser?"

"My old dresser, from when I was a kid."

"Good. We'll go get it tomorrow."

"It's oak. Big. Heavy. It's got a marble top."

"Perfect."

She looked around the room and then said dubiously, "I guess it could go there."

"Again, perfect. What else?"

"Pardon?"

"What other furniture is in the neighbor's barn?"

Ivy plopped down on the corner of the bed, one leg curled under her. "Well, there's a big rocking chair. It's wood and it has a caned seat and back. And the mirror that goes with the dresser. And the humidor. And my parent's sleigh—"

"Back up. Humidor?"

"It's a little cupboard, with a door, like a nightstand. It's lined with copper so cigars don't dry out."

"You smoked cigars in your wild youth?"

"Ick. No. When I was eleven, or maybe twelve, the humidor was out by the curb next door, with the trash. I didn't want it taken to the dump so I asked if I could keep it." She grinned. "I was inordinately proud of myself after I stripped off all the old orange paint and refinished it myself."

"Okay. The humidor. Now what was that about a sleigh?"

"A sleigh bed. One of those beds with a big, heavy curved headboard and footboard." She grinned. "When I was little I used to imagine that I was the Snow Queen sitting up against the headboard, with a driver standing in front of me and cracking a long whip over a matched set of four white horses."

"Would you rather we sleep in that bed, instead of this one?"

"Absolutely not. I love this huge bed. The sleigh bed is just an old-fashioned double."

"Good. Then the sleigh bed can be the first piece of furniture in the guest room. The guest room that's been empty since the house was built."

Ivy stared at him for a long moment. Then she spoke very slowly. "There's also a big piece of stained glass. Framed. A bird and flowers."

"All right."

"It's big."

"All right."

"It doesn't have to be displayed. We could store it out in the garage."

"We'll find a place for it."

She frowned. "You don't mind? Having your house full of unfamiliar furniture? Stuff you never chose?"

"You're missing the point, Ivy."

"I just don't want you to agree to something and then later find yourself wondering what on earth you've done."

"I asked you to move in with me. I didn't ask you to be a, a guest."

"But you didn't know what it meant, having me move in. You didn't know I had furniture."

"When I first asked you to move in, I thought you lived in East Montpelier. With a whole apartment full of furniture."

"Oh."

"I was asking you to blend our houses. To make a house that's ours. You didn't get it, did you?"

"Not till right now. No."

He turned away and slowly closed the dresser drawer. "How long will it be before you stop thinking 'your house', 'your bed'?"

"I've almost never used the word *our* in my whole life, Hugh."

Hugh turned to face her again across the wide bedroom. "That seems implausible. What about at the commune? Wasn't everything 'ours'?"

"No, it wasn't. Oddly enough. Usually it was 'the community'. The community plans this, or the community's gardens. It would have felt, I don't know, presumptuous for one person to say 'we' or 'ours'. Like he or she was trying to speak for the whole group."

Hugh crossed the room and stood in front of her. "Ivy, almost everything I owned burned. Neighbors carried some random things out onto the lawn before the fire trucks arrived. That wooden file cabinet in my office. Some stuff from the garage. Two paintings." He nodded toward the wall. "That's one."

Ivy looked past him at the large watercolor of irises. "I like that one."

"I lost everything else, including things I'd had since childhood." He reached down and shook her knee. "Ivy, I *want* the house to be full of things that have some personal history. I want to come home and open the front door and see a *home*."

Her eyes filled with tears. "Rats. I never used to cry, before you." She cleared her throat. "I didn't get what you meant, before. I didn't get that you want us to share a house that's full of your things and my things."

"How was that not clear?"

"I told you. I'm not good at this love thing."

"We'll both get better." He held out his hand. "Let's get outside in the fresh air."

****

Hugh and Ivy walked in silence through late afternoon shadows. There were people outdoors all over the neighborhood, sitting in their backyards, mowing their lawns, watching their children splashing and shrieking in pools. The air was full of the smells of cut grass, charcoal, grilled meat, and roasted corn.

"You're going to get tired of this, Hugh."

He glanced at her. "I like walking."

"No. Tired of me. I'm always skittering away. Always afraid to take the next step. You're going to come to the conclusion that I'm too much work. Or too much trouble."

For another half a block, they walked in silence, Hugh looking straight ahead with his face solemn. Then he sighed.

"I honestly can't see that happening." He looked down at her. "Getting tired of you. Not ever."

Ivy moved a few inches closer. When her hand brushed his wrist, he folded her fingers in his.

"You do realize, Ivy, that taking an afternoon walk together, hand in hand, is like wearing a sign: We Are A Couple."

"That's okay. Now that I've had sufficient time to mull."

"Mull."

"And ponder. Now that I've mulled and pondered, I'm okay with it."

"Heads up."

"What?"

"You are about to be introduced for the first time as

one half of a couple."

"That's what you're going to say? This is Ivy, she's one—"

"Mr. MacDougal! We usually see you running by like a man being chased by demons. But you're actually strolling!"

There was a large woman approaching them, swathed from her many chins to her chubby ankles in yards of striped gauzy fabric. A lean silky dog at her side contemplated Hugh and Ivy with mild interest.

"It's nice to stroll for a change." Hugh's fingers tightened. "Ivy, Mrs. Thompson lives across the street from us. Poppy, I'd like you to meet my sweetheart, Ivy Pritchard."

The woman's eyes glittered with curiosity. "Ivy. So you're the reason for our Mr. MacDougal's happy face. And his strolling. Delighted to meet you."

"I'm pleased to meet you too, Mrs. Thompson."

"Poppy. Please!"

"That's an elegant dog, Mrs.—Poppy. Is it a Saluki? Or Borzoi?"

The other woman beamed approvingly. "Borzoi, yes. Almost no one around here knows those breeds. Everyone thinks Anastasia is a hairy greyhound."

"May I pet her?"

"Of course! She loves people!"

Ivy held out her hand and the dog regally lowered its long nose for a sniff.

"You're a beauty, you are. And you feel so good." She looked up. "Anastasia is a fine name for a Russian dog."

"Yes, indeed. Her father was Rasputin. But for some reason the bitch, her mother, was Valencia. Go figure!"

The woman's chins quivered as she threw back her head and laughed. Then she beamed at Ivy. "I like you! Most Vermonters like retrievers. Or big drooling breeds like Bernese Mountain Dogs."

"There certainly are a lot of those around."

"I know! Slobber and hip dysplasia and all. When everyone could have clean beauties like Anastasia here. There's just no accounting for taste."

"Hugh used to have a West Highland Terrier."

Mrs. Thompson nodded sagely. "A good choice, Hugh. A good choice indeed."

"Well." Hugh gently propelled Ivy forward. "We'll let you and Anastasia get back to your walk. Nice seeing you."

As they moved away, the woman called after them, "I hope to see you both at the Labor Day barbecue!"

"I'm sorry I mentioned Laird, Hugh. I didn't mean to bring back sad memories."

"That was fine. But how on earth did you remember his breed? And his name?"

"I honestly think I remember every single thing you've ever said to me. Or near me."

There was silence again for several steps.

"Do you remember everything Molly says? Or Charlie?"

"No."

"So it's not just unusually good memory."

"No."

Hugh and Ivy moved onto a lawn so a jogger pushing a stroller could pass them.

"I remember what you were wearing the first time I saw you."

"Too easy, Hugh. I wear pretty much the same thing

on every bird walk."

"No. It was still cold."

"Oh. That's right. Eagles on the ice. And your Barred Owls."

"Black wind pants. Green shell over a blue fleece thing with a high collar. Green hat and mittens." His thumb caressed the back of her hand. "You took off your mittens when you put on sunscreen, and you had a Band-Aid on your left thumb."

"Goodness. Now I feel silly."

"Why?"

"For rejecting the word couple. What with my remembering your every word and you remembering my Band-Aid, for Pete's sake, we were a couple before we even knew it."

"I knew pretty early. Well, I hoped." He gave an exaggerated sigh. "It was an uphill climb getting you on board, though."

"I'm glad you persisted."

"In the face of considerable resistance and rejection."

"In the face of resistance and rejection. Yes." She smiled at him. "I like *sweetheart*, by the way."

"It seemed warmer than significant other."

"Or posselqueue."

"What?"

"P.O.S.S.L.Q. Persons of opposite sex sharing living quarters."

"Good god. Did you just make that up?"

"I think the Census Bureau did."

"Good god."

They moved off the sidewalk again to make room for an elderly couple, the man using a walker. Hugh nodded and murmured, "Commodore. Mrs. Peat" and the pair nodded in return.

"So you do know your neighbors."

"Of course I do."

"Molly said you never come to community events."

"Well, I've been here for several years. I've never worked at making friends but I know people's names." Hugh glanced back over his shoulder at the two slow-moving people. "I'm not a hundred percent sure he really was a commodore. That might be part of his dementia. So I'm always in a quandary when I meet them. If I call him by the title, am I being condescending, the way people often are to the elderly? But if I don't call him Commodore and he really was one, it might be disrespectful."

"Both he and his wife looked comfortable with the title."

"True."

"Your neighbor Poppy, by the way, has the largest breasts I've ever seen in my entire life."

"Impressive, aren't they? Sometimes she stands at her front gate with her folded arms resting on that huge shelf, and absolutely nothing jiggles or shifts. Her undergarments have to be marvels of engineering." Hugh looked sideways at her, his eyes crinkling. "The kids next door call her T-Cubed. Three Ts. For Ten Ton Titties."

Ivy gave a little snort of laughter. "That's awful!"

"Descriptive, though." He raised her hand to his mouth and kissed her fingers. "You looked like you liked that dog. Anastasia. The dog liked you too."

"I've always gotten on well with animals."

"We could get a dog. Maybe several."

Ivy kept her eyes straight ahead and her face calm. "Cool idea, Hugh."

"I take it back. Not several dogs. But definitely one. For the kids. One dog, several kids."

She glanced at him. The corner of his mouth was twitching.

"You are teasing, right?"

"In part."

"Let's not talk about dogs or babies today. Let's not talk about them for, say, one year."

"Six months."

"Eight months. My final offer."

He raised his arm and looked at his watch.

"It's September 18. Next May 18, we will sit down and talk about bringing babies and dogs into *our* house."

"Future planning."

"Yes."

"Like a couple."

"Yes, my sweetheart. Like a couple."

****

"Ahh. Olives and grease and cheese and oil. I am one happy woman." Ivy popped the last bit of pizza into her mouth.

"Grease and oil both, huh?"

"Both."

"Tell me more about the stained glass bird."

"It's mostly flowers, actually. With one bird. One of my jobs at the commune was helping TreeSoul."

Hugh raised one eyebrow.

"That probably wasn't her original name. She was the herbalist. She was in her eighties when I first met her, and she died during my tenth year there." Ivy looked out the kitchen window to the trees hung with bird feeders.

226

"There were so many things that tiny, frail-looking old woman could do. So many things she knew. She was an amazing birder. Naturalist, really. All kinds of wildlife. And of course an exceptional gardener." She gave a little laugh as she remembered. "And she could bring down a tree with a chainsaw faster and neater than anyone. It was as if she talked with the tree and explained what she needed and then the tree just laid itself right down where she wanted it."

Hugh leaned forward and poured a bit more wine into her glass.

"Thanks. And she made stained glass artwork, to sell and to give to her friends." Ivy's eyes were suddenly somber. "One day, a few months before she died, TreeSoul said she had something bird-related for me. It was leaning against a wall in a dark corner, so I couldn't tell at first what it was. I knew it had to be a piece of stained glass, but I…"

She took a sip of wine, her eyes glistening with unshed tears. "I can't imagine how long it must have taken her, Hugh. It has literally hundreds of pieces. Individual leaves, petals on the flowers, blades of grass… Well, you'll see. She said it's a picture of a hummingbird but the bird is just a tiny part. It's a whole garden. It almost feels like you can walk right into it. It's the most special thing I've ever owned."

"What about hanging it from our bedroom ceiling, a few feet in from the window? It'll catch the morning light."

"That is a lovely idea, Hugh. Perfect." The far-away look left her eyes. "It's been several hours since I've said it. I love you, Hugh. I love you immensely."

"I love you immensely too." He stood up. "Let's call

227

around and get someone to move your beautiful hummingbird garden here. And the rest of your stuff. To our house."

"Good idea." She wiped her greasy fingers. "Pizza was a good idea, too."

"Here's another one. I'm on a roll."

"Yes?"

"Let's see if we can borrow Charlie's boat and spend tomorrow on the water."

A slow smile spread over her face. "That sounds perfectly wonderful, Hugh."

****

Ivy rolled to her side and looked at his sleeping face. "Hugh?" She traced his close-cut beard with her fingers. "Wake up, love. You said you wanted to see this."

He made a rumbling noise.

She traced his mustache and then his lips, watching with amusement as he barely moved his mouth to mutter, "Wha' time?"

"A little past dawn."

The first light of the day had reached halfway across the patio, gilding the bamboo chairs and changing the bricks from brown to red.

Hugh groaned and rolled toward her without opening his eyes. "Do I have time to pee?"

"I'd hate for you to miss it. It'll only be a few minutes more."

Light touched the bottom of the broad window.

Hugh sighed and opened his eyes. "All right. I'm awake."

They sat up against the headboard and Hugh put his arm around her.

"Grab a fistful."

"What? Oh."

They both yanked on the light quilt, pulling it free from the bottom of the bed, and he tucked it around their shoulders.

"Much better, Hugh. A little tent of warmth."

"Body warmth. Warm bodies. Mmm. Warm bare body."

"No distractions. It's almost time."

The morning light touched a corner of the hanging stained glass, and colored shapes appeared on the wall, shifting and dancing.

As they watched, the slanting sunlight illuminated a quarter of the stained glass. Then half.

The whole bedroom was full of dancing lights.

And the glass garden came alive. Emerald-colored leaves. Jade green leaves. Leaves made of such dark green glass they were almost black. Lemon yellow lilies. Pink roses. Deep purple irises. Rich blue delphiniums and pale blue forget-me-nots.

At last the light touched the hummingbird in the upper corner. In an instant, its throat changed from deepest black to brilliant crimson. The shimmering green wings, made of tiny triangular chips of glass, looked as if they were in motion.

Ivy laughed in delight. "There it is, Hugh. Oh, there it is! TreeSoul's wonderful present to us, to both of us."

"A house-warming present."

"Yes, Hugh. For us and our house."

Chapter Twenty-Eight

When the gray and yellow bird finally tumbled out of the winds, it was on a rocky island, surrounded by the cries of gulls and seabirds. The exhausted bird fluttered toward a patch of evergreens. But before its feet even touched a branch, there was an explosion of movement and panic. The bird tried to fly, to escape, but it was knocked to the hard ground and held there by something not yet clearly seen, something large and furry and terrifying. The warbler struggled, beating its wings furiously, twisting this way and that. Just as the cat lunged with its other paw, the bird broke free and rocketed several yards across the lawn, whirling, flailing, uncontrolled.

The cat yowled and leapt after its prey. But it abruptly stopped and held up its right paw. It shook its paw, put weight on it, lifted it again. The warbler flew to the very highest part of a nearby pine while the cat yowled again in frustration, trying to retract its claws, trying to get rid of the little plastic and metal device. After several minutes, the geolocator dropped to the ground.

Chapter Twenty-Nine

Hugh reached up to unfasten the boat straps on his side of the car. "Ivy, I just had a thought."

"What's your thought, sweet man?"

"Let's go to Newfoundland."

"What?!"

"When we picked up the boat, Charlie said there was a report of a Grace's Warbler up in Newfoundland several days ago. It must be our bird, don't you think?"

"Maybe. Probably! It does seem unlikely that two of them would end up so far out of range."

"So let's go. Let's see for ourselves where that confused little bird ended up."

"That's a long trip, Hugh."

"Not by air."

"You're thinking a few days without work? Just the two of us?"

"Yes. Soon. Before it starts getting cold up there."

Ivy bent and peered through the few inches between the canoe and the roof of the car. "Do you know what I'm doing right now?"

"No idea."

"I'm beaming at your shirt front."

"My shirt front appreciates the attention."

There was a whirring sound as they pulled the straps off the boat.

"You think Molly would cover for you in the store?"

"I'll call her as soon as we get home. What about your work?"

"The problem clients accepted the revised plans and the builder goes into high gear tomorrow. I don't have a meeting with new clients for almost two weeks."

"Excellent." Ivy rounded the car with a little skipping step. "A vacation with you!"

Hugh crouched by the back fender to untie a rope. "Have you done much canoeing?"

"Zilch. There were kayaks on the pond at the commune, and a rowboat. But no canoes."

"Then I'll take the stern first. All you have to do is paddle." He stood. "Coming back we can switch if you want to. One, two, three. Lift."

Ivy braced her legs and heaved, and then gasped. "Oh! When you and Charlie lifted it onto the car, I thought you were showing off your manly muscles. But it's not very heavy."

"Nope. Big, wide, sturdy and stable—but not heavy."

They lowered the boat into the water.

"Stable, huh? I thought canoes were really tippy."

"Not this one. Get in."

She cautiously climbed in, grabbed both gunnels, and made her way to the front. She didn't dare turn around but she felt when Hugh got in and sat down, and then they were moving away from shore.

"Do I do one stroke on the left and then one on the right?"

"Nope. Paddle on whichever side feels comfortable for as long as you want. Switch sides when you feel like it."

"Oh! This is easy!"

She heard his deep chuckle behind her.

There were several other boats on the reservoir, mostly small fishing boats. Close to the opposite shore, a noisy group of young kayakers called out to each other, laughing and splashing.

Ivy forgot all about looking for birds. She watched her wooden paddle dipping into the still water, watched the sun sparkling on the ripples, felt the smooth forward movement of the boat.

"This is the inlet, ahead. That's where Charlie and Sean went, the day they found the warbler."

"Oh. Yes."

He steered them into the quiet stream. Almost immediately, the kayakers' laughter and shouts faded. Trees grew down to the water on both sides, and the temperature was several degrees cooler.

"You know, Ivy. This vacation can be like a honeymoon."

Ivy's rhythm faltered. When her paddle made a loud splash, a slender crow-sized bird took off from a low branch a few yards ahead of them.

"A Green Heron! Drat! If I hadn't splashed, we would could have had a great look."

"It's flying upstream and we're going upstream. We'll have another chance."

"Good."

"Ship your oar."

"Pardon?"

"Put your paddle across the front of the canoe and just sit. I'll keep us moving."

The big canoe glided slowly upstream. As they rounded a bend, Hugh and Ivy saw the heron on a fallen log, green and chestnut plumage glowing in a shaft of sunlight. As they watched, the bird broke off a tiny piece of twig and placed it in a pool of water separated from the main channel by an exposed tree root. Several minutes passed. Then the heron lunged forward, extending its neck and stabbing the water with its bill. It lifted its head, shaking water into a wreath of glittering droplets, holding tight to a struggling fish.

"I've never seen that."

"Can't hear you."

Ivy turned her head just a little. "I've read about Green Herons using bait to catch fish but I've never seen it."

The heron tipped its head up, made little movements with its bill, then jerked its head and swallowed.

"Yum. Sushi." Ivy picked up her paddle and the heron lifted off, again flying upstream. "Silly bird. If it would just turn and fly back over us, we wouldn't disturb it again."

Hugh steered them back into the main channel. Twice more they came close to the heron, and twice more it took off and flew ahead of them.

"I think Charlie and Sean found the warbler near here."

"White pines. Could be."

"Should we keep going?"

"Let's."

Ivy was again mesmerized, watching the reflections of trees in the still water, turning her head to see the ripples from her paddle. The woods were very quiet, with occasional tapping sounds from woodpeckers and sapsuckers and the distant caw of a crow.

"I think we've reached our turn-around spot."

Ahead of them, the stream was blocked by a large

fallen tree, upturned roots on one side, topmost branches far up the opposite bank. When Hugh angled the boat parallel to the tree, Ivy lifted her legs to her chest and cautiously swung around to face him.

"You rarely speak without thinking first, Hugh. What were thinking when you mentioned a honeymoon?"

"At that moment? That a first vacation together, for many couples, is their honeymoon."

"Oh."

"But then, while we were paddling, I began thinking it might be a good idea. To think of it as a honeymoon. You were anxious about dating, anxious about moving in. If we take a vacation and call it a honeymoon, perhaps you won't feel so anxious when we start talking about marriage."

"Marriage, huh? You're thinking we'll drift into it? As the next logical step?"

"Something like that."

She stared at him for a long moment.

"Do you remember on our first date, Hugh? When we got to your house and sat in the driveway for a while?"

"I will never forget."

"It was smart of you to want me to choose. To want me to be clear about going inside with you."

"It wasn't smart. It was zero confidence."

"Well, it was still a good idea. It felt wonderful. Deciding. I think sex was so amazing for us, right from that first time, because both of us equally wanted and both of us equally opted."

"I agree."

They sat quiet, Hugh making small movements with

his paddle and Ivy studying his face.

"I don't want to just drift into marriage, Hugh. I want to be as one hundred percent sure as I was that day out in your car."

"I'm willing to wait."

"Good." Her face relaxed. "Because which would be better? Me standing in front of you and saying I DO with loud conviction? Or me mumbling 'Sure. Why not? It's the next logical step'?"

The corners of Hugh's mouth twitched. "Again. I'm willing to wait."

Ivy cautiously stretched her legs out in front of her. "I've drifted most of my life, Hugh. I've very rarely opted."

"You've said that before, Ivy, but I find it hard to believe. You own a business. You went to college. You've done interesting things in your life."

"I drifted off to college to satisfy my parents." She gave a little shrug. "And to get away from them. I didn't have any major in mind. Going to college was just what the offspring of high school principals did.

"I drifted into sociology because one semester those were the classes that fit around birding. I drifted off to the commune because my professor suggested it and I didn't have anything else planned. I never intended to stay but I was there for twelve years, perfectly happy planting veggie seeds in the spring and harvesting squashes in the fall and living in the tree house they gave me and eating whatever there was to eat without planning ahead for one single meal.

"And I certainly never decided, hey, I think I'd like to go live in a mall. It was just easier than finding an apartment. And I never thought I'd own a store but then my dad died and I had money just when the guy who owned the store needed cash. I think I've always lived day to day. Drifted. And I've always been happy about it.

"But marrying you, Hugh, being with you for our lifetimes, is more important than anything I've ever done. I don't want to drift into it just because you're nudging me and I love you and it would be easy to go along."

"A canoe isn't a good place to do what I want us to do right now."

She looked around. "If we get just a little closer to the bank, we can both get out and—"

"Ticks."

"Beg pardon?"

"No sex in the woods. Ticks."

"Ick. Okay. Hold the boat steady. I'm going to very carefully wiggle and crawl toward you."

"This is a very stable boat."

"So you say." Ivy slid onto her knees, grabbed both gunnels and inched forward. "We can have one long consuming kiss to tide us over until we get home, and then let's change places and paddle back. I want to try steering."

When she reached the middle of the boat, she turned sideways, wiggled her bottom onto the central seat, lifted her legs over, and again slid to her knees.

"Tada. I'm almost there and I haven't tipped us into the water."

Hugh's dark eyes were alive with laughter. He spread his knees and Ivy crept closer until she could put her hands on his warm chest.

"Keep hold of that branch, Hugh."

"Will do."

"One kiss."

"Will do…. Hmm… More later."

Ivy shuffled backwards, her hands gripping the sides of the boat. "Okay. Now I'll grab hold of the branch and you can move."

Hugh stood up, calmly walked the length of the boat, and took his seat in the bow.

Ivy let out an explosive spurt of laughter. "You rat. You could have stopped me at any time during my whole crawling, squirming and wiggling routine."

He picked up the paddle. "I told you. This is a very stable boat."

****

"Ivy? Come in here, sweetheart." Hugh was leaning back in his office chair, his arms behind his head, his long legs stretched out in front of him. "Look at this."

On the screen was a line of cottages set back from a rocky cliff with gray and white waves visible in the background, along with hundreds of whirling birds.

"That looks wonderful, Hugh."

"The last cottage is available for a week starting Thursday."

"This coming Thursday? Four days from now?"

"After that, the place closes down until next summer."

"I'd…" She looked back at his computer. "That looks wonderful, Hugh."

"Good. I just reserved it. I was afraid it might be gone if we waited." He twirled the chair around to face her. "There's an afternoon flight to Montreal with a connection for a little local airport. We'd get in by seven and get to the cottage by eight-thirty at the latest. What did Molly say?"

"Good news and bad news." She picked up the rocking chair and moved it so close that their knees were touching. "She can work every day starting Friday afternoon. She needs Thursday off to be with her grandkids, and she won't be in until around noon on Friday because of a dentist appointment."

"So we can't leave Thursday. Can you leave as soon as Molly gets there on Friday?"

"Definitely."

"So we'll be just a day late."

She leaned forward and put her hand on his thigh. "You go up Thursday. I'll join you Friday evening."

"Being in Newfoundland, alone, while you're here in Vermont, seems a bit contrary to the whole idea of a shared vacation."

"The cottage is there, Hugh. Already reserved. And the ocean's there. And the birds. And if you go birding all day Friday, you can show me what's what. I know nothing about sea birds."

He gazed at her for a long moment. "Groceries."

"Beg pardon?"

"While I'm alone on Friday I'll buy groceries for the week. We won't have to waste any time when we're together."

Ivy looked at him sternly. "Tell me that you'll also go birding."

"I'll also go birding." He turned back to his computer. "I'm going to nail down our flights."

As Ivy turned to leave the room, Hugh added, "I'll buy groceries and I'll go birding. But mostly I'll be thinking about honeymooning with you. Anticipating."

She grinned.

"Well, right now, Hugh, I'm going to bed. I'll be waiting for you. Anticipating."

"I'll be right in."

Chapter Thirty

Two days after losing the geolocator, the Grace's Warbler left the cliffs by the ocean and resumed its journey, continuing on the path that had brought it all the way from Mexico to Newfoundland. The night sky was full of migrants, all heading south. Some of the birds would be seen by the FATSO birders in just a few days: American Pipits, Horned Larks, Yellow-rumped Warblers. Perhaps one or two of the migrating American Golden Plovers would delight Vermont birders by veering inland instead of hugging the coast. Kestrels and Merlins patrolled the flocks of migrants, picking off the slower, the weaker and the unlucky, taking on fuel for their own journeys.

The small gray and yellow bird was caught in the swirl of southbound birds. At last, it surrendered to what was easier. The Grace's Warbler turned around and headed south. It might not ever end up in an area where others of its species lived and courted and mated and raised young. But, for the first time since May, there was that possibility.

Chapter Thirty-One

The sky was just beginning to get light toward the east when Ivy saw Hugh's long body coming along the gravel walk. She left her luggage on the cottage porch and ran to meet him.

"Hugh!"

He turned and caught her and for a brief moment his arms tightened around her almost to the point of pain. Then he loosened his grip and pushed her away.

"What are you doing here? Where were you?"

She took a step backwards. "Pardon?"

"You should have been here last night. Where have you been all this time?" He was holding himself stiffly, his eyes bloodshot and wary.

"I told you. In the message."

"You didn't tell me. I didn't get a message."

"I couldn't get you on your cell so I talked to a man named Chuck. He said he'd leave a note in the message box."

"I don't know anything about a message box."

"I told him to let you know I'd be hours late."

"Why?"

"Many things." Ivy was frowning. "Engine trouble made us late leaving Montreal. Then when we got up here to Newfoundland, the shuttle was done for the night. One of the airport security men gave me a ride. Gave us a ride. Three of us. I was the farthest so he dropped me off last."

"Why didn't you come get me?"

Ivy began to feel both defensive and irritated. "I didn't know which cottage we were in, Hugh. And the office was closed so I couldn't ask. And you didn't leave a light on."

"You knew we had the last cottage."

She turned and pointed. There were seven identical little buildings in a row, a gap, and then three larger ones.

"The last one before the gap? Or the really last one? I didn't want to go pounding on the wrong door at 2:30 in the morning."

"The three big ones are private."

"I didn't know that."

"Where have you been since 2:30?"

She made a vague gesture. "Over there. The first cabin. It's being painted. It was open. I napped on the bed. What on earth is wrong with you?"

"I thought you weren't coming."

Her jaw dropped. "What?"

Hugh lifted his chin and almost spat out his next words. "I thought you weren't coming. I thought it was over."

"God in heaven, Hugh." She stared at him, her face white. When he turned his head away, toward the gray ocean, she took another step backwards. "I am going to get my bags. I'm going to put them in our cottage. The last cottage of the first seven cottages, but not really the last cottage." She pointed toward the entrance. "Someone just pulled up at the office. You are going to go, right now, and ask about the message box."

Ivy retrieved her luggage and was heading for the last of the little cottages when Hugh was suddenly beside her, his fingers brushing hers as he took the handle of the rolling bag.

"Message box." He stopped by a square post with the number seven painted on it in the same bright blue as the shutters on the last cottage. He unlatched the top, reached into a small cavity and took out a folded piece of paper.

Ivy waited while he read the note.

He met her eyes. "Thank you for this."

Ivy didn't answer.

"I didn't think you were coming."

"I find that impossible to believe. That you thought for even one second that I would just not show up." She turned abruptly toward the ocean. "I don't want to go inside. I want us to sit on that bench. It will be easier to talk with... with space around us."

Hugh opened the cottage door, shoved her bag inside, and then walked beside her toward the cliff and the ocean. They sat down in silence, both facing the sea, inches between their stiff bodies.

Thin remnants of the night's fog drifted across the cliffs. Wind off the ocean brought a strong ammonia smell from a bird-covered sea stack separated from the headland by a narrow strip of water. The air was full of the sounds of seabirds waking to another day of fishing and feeding young and feuding.

Ivy took a deep breath and let it out slowly. "It would have made sense, Hugh, if you had spent the night worrying about a plane crash. Or the shuttle, from the airport to here. If you'd taken the rental car and gone looking for wreckage. Or... or if you'd made up a scenario about the whole airport being under siege by terrorists. Even that might have made sense. But it made absolutely no sense to worry that I might not be coming. No sense at all."

"I checked the news, Ivy. There was nothing about plane crashes." He tightened his fingers around the edge of the bench, his knuckles white. "And it did make sense. It made perfect sense. You were uncomfortable talking about marriage but that didn't stop me. I kept pushing you."

"When, Hugh? When did you push me about marriage?"

"I brought it up when we were canoeing. I talked about this trip as our honeymoon. And then Wednesday. When the garbage truck hit the mailbox. I said we'd have to put both our names on the new one."

"God in heaven, Hugh."

He kept talking, his voice flat and dogged. "All night long I kept thinking the same thing, over and over. Endless loop. My marriage to Elaine ended because I didn't know how to love her the way she wanted. Physically. And now I was losing you, and the only reason I could come up with is that I haven't been able to love you the way you need either. Emotionally this time."

He stared out to sea and Ivy stared at his profile. When she finally started talking, her lips were stiff, her voice tight. "The first time you told me about your burns, Hugh, you said you didn't want other people to pity you. But right now I think you would be perfectly happy if the whole wide world was right out there in front of us, with every single human pointing right at you and pitying you. Because they'd all be supporting what you're already feeling. You are completely engrossed in pitying yourself."

He flinched.

"Oh god. I'm sorry, Hugh. No, I'm not. Not for what I said. But I'm sorry for the way I said it. I'm tired and hungry and angry. And hurt…. I have something to say, but I need a few seconds to figure out how to say it without being nasty again."

Hugh leaned forward, his back rigid, his head bent, his arms stiff.

"Okay." Ivy lifted her shoulders and inhaled. "You were wrong about you and Elaine, and you're wrong about you and me."

"I know that. I just said that. I made mistakes with both of you."

She ignored his comment. "You're an honest person. But for years you've tormented yourself with a falsehood about your marriage. You say you didn't understand your wife and that's why your marriage failed. That is absolute hooey. It wouldn't have made one iota of difference if you had understood. If Elaine had written you a script that told you exactly what she wanted. You still wouldn't have met her needs."

His head came up.

"What, Hugh? Would you have shoved her against a wall? Would you have forced her even when she was saying no? Of course you wouldn't. Not ever. That woman wanted a Neanderthal and you're not a Neanderthal and you couldn't have even pretended to be a Neanderthal. Not even if you knew it might have saved your marriage. End of story. I'm tired of hearing about it."

There was a long silence. When she started talking again, her voice was gentler. "I am absolutely sure that you showed your wife what most women long for.

Thoughtful, creative, loving sex. Just what you've shown me. But something in her couldn't respond. The marriage was doomed from day one. But that doomed, long-ago marriage is still so important that last night it blotted out a fundamental truth about you and me. A truth you should have…" She had to clear her throat before continuing. "You should know by now how much I love you. You should know it absolutely, with every fiber of your being." Her voice rose. "You should have trusted me! You should have known there was no way on earth I would just leave you up here!"

"I—"

"I'm talking!—Sorry. I wanted to stay calm and rational."

A line of cormorants flew in front of them, only a foot or two above the waves, their long skinny necks extended.

A pea-green van appeared from nowhere and pulled up close to the bench. The van's door opened and a man in a birding vest jumped down. Ivy turned her head. She could see people inside, standing up, gathering equipment, moving toward the door. As they climbed out, the smell of coffee from their travel mugs mingled with the bird smells in the cool morning air.

Hugh loosened his grip on the edge of the bench and slid back. "Are you done now?"

"I… Yes. I guess that's all."

The trip leader raised his voice. "Great to see you all up and eager so early this morning. It will be worth it, I promise you."

One of the birders looked at the sky and groaned loudly. "It's barely dawn, for Christ's sake."

The leader gave a hearty laugh. "You were all

forewarned. This trip is not for the faint of heart, the faint of mind, or the faint of body. If we don't end up with one hundred species today it will not be for lack of trying!" He looked around at his group. "These cabins are owned by a friend of mine and he's getting breakfast ready right now. We've got a half hour or so to scan the cliffs and the ocean from here to the lighthouse." He threw open the back doors of the van so people could get backpacks and tripods. Birders started walking by, several muttering apologies as they passed the couple on the bench. The guide called out, "There's no railing so watch your footing. We don't want to lose anybody into the sea."

Hugh dragged in a deep breath and straightened his back. "I have always felt the weight of my personal responsibility for my own future. That weight was heaviest during my marriage but it's always been there. Always." He shifted on the bench and Ivy felt the warmth of his arm against hers. "Starting way back in fifth grade, when I figured out what I had to do to be on the track team by the time I reached high school. I was a scrawny kid. It wasn't easy."

"But you did it. You got on the track team. Varsity."

Hugh glanced at her. "You remembered that."

"Of course."

"I planned and worked at everything, Ivy. Sports. Academics. I even remember making a list of what I had to change about myself before I could ask out a girl I liked." He gave a little shrug. "That one didn't work."

A large white bird with black wing tips made a circle in front of them, stopped in mid-air, tucked its long wings close to its body, and dove straight down into the water.

"I lived for what my life was going to be like *someday*," Hugh continued. "Someday in the future. After I got on the football team. After I started dating Peg or Marilyn or Samantha. After I got my degree. After I had a practice. When I had a wife and children."

"Yo, gang! Move over here so you're not blocking that couple's view." The birding group stopped several yards from Hugh and Ivy. "Northern Gannets might be the showiest birds that nest here but they're definitely not alone. We'll be looking for Common Murres, Thick-billed Murres, Black Guillemots and Razorbills. Maybe a puffin or two, if we're lucky."

"Hugh. Which of those species did you see yesterday?"

"Not now. Later." He turned to face her, his bony knee warm and tight against her thigh. "Ivy, you've said you never had a real sense of the future, that you just drifted. I've always been the opposite. I almost never had *now*. Not until you. When we were walking down from the ledge after our first time, I told you that I felt real, that I was in the present, that I had almost never experienced the present, not with that kind of intensity. That continues to be the great gift you give me. You give me the intense joy of this moment. Every single day, almost since we met."

"That's a lovely thing to say."

"It's a lovely thing to feel…. You might be… I have to reword that. You are right. I think you're right, Ivy, about my marriage to Elaine."

She made a noncommittal noise.

"I think it's true that we were a bad match. I wasn't what she wanted. She wasn't what I wanted either. I didn't know it at the time but she really wasn't."

Ivy waited.

After a long moment of silence, he inhaled again, pressing his back against the bench and lifting his face to the breeze.

"A weight's off them?"

"What?"

"Your shoulders. Do you feel that a weight is off your shoulders?"

"Oh!" He looked startled. "Yes, actually. I do. Right now I do. But… " The corner of his mouth twisted up. "But I might relapse from time to time."

"We'll figure it out."

A middle-aged man, unshaven and with his hair standing on end, hurried past the bench, clutching his binoculars and looking harried.

"One clarification. You said I showed Elaine what you and I have in bed. That's not true. It wasn't the same with her. Sex with you has been extraordinary from the very first."

The man glanced at them, startled, and quickly looked away.

"Sorry, Ivy. I didn't mean to broadcast that."

She surprised them both with a spurt of laughter. "It's fine. When he gets back in the van, he'll tell his seatmate what he overheard and they'll both chuckle. It'll make him feel better about having to take a potty break and ending up last in line." She looked down at the tanned hand so close to her on the bench. When she touched his knuckles, he turned his hand over and she laid her palm on his and they tightened their fingers. "I love your hands, Hugh. I am so relieved to feel your hand touching me right now that I feel lightheaded."

"That could be sleep-deprivation. Or hunger."

"No!" Her eyes were fierce as she looked into his face. "It's relief, Hugh. And such a huge surge of love for you that I almost can't breathe."

"I love you too. I should have trusted what we have."

"You should have."

They both turned and looked toward the ocean, their bodies now close together, their hands tight.

"Oh. The owner of these cabins told me that one of the guests found a geolocator day before yesterday."

"No!"

"He already called VCE and he's waiting for instructions on what to do with the thing."

"That's exciting, Hugh. It has to be our warbler!"

"It might not even be from a warbler."

"I'm sure it's our warbler." She lifted his hand and kissed it. "Absolutely sure."

He stroked her hand with a finger. "I spent a lot of time yesterday watching gannets."

"They're bigger than I thought."

"Their wingspan is almost six feet."

"Yikes."

"The white ones are the adults. You probably knew that. With the dark wing tips and orangey color on the head. The darker ones are this year's young. And the mottled ones are in their second or third summer." His face looked relaxed for the first time. "I studied the big fat Sibley guide coming up in the plane—"

"Of course you did."

"—so I was able to recognize the young of several species." He caressed the back of her hand with his thumb. "All that time watching young birds got me thinking about children."

Ivy's fingers twitched.

"I know. We agreed to wait to talk about kids. But I need to say this right now. I realized yesterday afternoon that I'm not as eager to have children as I thought. I'm not sure I want anything—kids or dogs or anything—cutting into the time we have with each other. Not yet."

The diving gannets blurred.

"Don't cry, Ivy. I just wanted you to know that we can talk about kids sometime, if you want to, but I won't be pressuring you."

She nodded wordlessly.

"So what were you thinking, all alone in that empty cabin, smelling the wet paint and waiting for daybreak?" He gave her a little smile. "All the time I was alone in our cabin, awake, unhappy, being an idiot?"

She traced the valleys between his knuckles with a fingertip. Her voice was low and hesitant. "Well, partly I was thinking that when we get home, Hugh, we should have a serious conversation about logistics."

"Logistics."

"Yes. We should get out our checkbooks and bank statements and tax forms, spread them out all over the kitchen table, and—"

Hugh interrupted her, disbelief and amusement in his eyes. "I was thinking about making babies with you and you were thinking about bank statements?"

"I'm, um, easing into things."

His expression changed. "Oh."

She stared down at their hands. "And I was thinking that we should discuss things like property taxes, and gas and electricity and fuel oil. Who pays what."

"All right."

"And maybe even meet with a financial counselor.

If that seems like a good idea to you."

"It does."

"And we should talk about wills. And how we could make medical decisions for each other, in case of…" Her voice broke. She tightened her fingers. "Basically, Hugh, I was thinking about marriage. What it entails. The nitty-gritty."

"The nitty-gritty of marriage."

She met his eyes. "Hugh. I very much want to be your wife. Immediately. As soon as we get home…. Oh don't! If you get teary, I'll start bawling and we'll be a real distraction for those birders."

"I truly did not expect this conversation to include that."

"Well, unlike you, I spent the whole time we've been apart looking forward to seeing you, lonely for you. Loving you so much it hurt." She tried a grin. "It wasn't me who spent one whole night obsessing over something that couldn't possibly happen."

"So you're saying yes now because you feel sorry for me?"

"Yes. That's exactly it, Hugh. As Sean would say, *nailed* it! You being absolutely awesome in every way, every minute of every day, for months now, just didn't do it for me. But a few truly idiotic behaviors and I'm willing to commit to you for the rest of my life." She let go of his hand, grabbed his knee, and shook it. "I decided to say yes, to marry you if you want me, yesterday afternoon. When I had absolutely no idea you were up here morphing into a moron."

"If I want you." Hugh slid his hands into her wind-tossed curls. "*That's* moronic."

She made a little sound of protest when he pulled

away after only a few seconds.

"More later, Ivy. In private."

"A lot more." She touched her fingertips to her own mouth and then his. "Endless kisses. As befits a honeymooning couple."

The birding group started back in their direction, and Ivy recognized the man who had been the last to go out to the cliff. Now he was walking with a woman whose shirt, hat, and binoculars matched his. Ivy beamed up at them.

"We're getting married! We're going to spend our lives birding and loving and being married!"

"Birding and extraordinary sex." The man winked. "Works for us." After a few steps, he turned back toward Hugh and Ivy. "Be sure to look at the little rock straight out from the twelfth orange marker. There are two Atlantic Puffins there."

"Thank you so much! That would be another life list bird for both of us!"

"Consider it a wedding present."

Hugh leaned his head against Ivy's and murmured, "Birding and sex. Works for them."

"Us too."

"We might have a rocky road sometimes. You know that, Ivy."

"I know." She smiled. "We'll also have rocky road."

"I just said that."

"You said a rocky road. I said rocky road. The flavor. Rich and sweet. With wonderful chunks. You and I are going to have richness and sweetness, Hugh. With chunks of extra deliciousity."

He raised one eyebrow.

"That's a word."

He said nothing.

"Then it should be a word."

"All right, Ivy. My sweetheart, my love, my fiancée. My deliciousity. We've got the cottage for six more nights. It's supposed to rain this afternoon and probably all of tomorrow but then it'll be sunny. What should we do?"

"You're the expert at planning for the future, Hugh. Come up with a plan. Then I will exercise my rights as equal partner in this relationship and I'll vote it up or down."

He stroked her cheek. "There's a continental breakfast in the office, and I gather that it's starting early today because of the bird tour. I suggest we get something in our bellies and then go get the scope and tripod and binoculars and walk the cliff trail and do some serious birding. Then at noon or so, I suggest we drive about mile up the road and pig out on seafood." His voice roughened. "And then I suggest that we come back and spend all afternoon, all evening, and all night in bed. All day tomorrow too if it's still raining. As befits a honeymooning couple."

She looked thoughtful for a long moment. Then she nodded briskly. "I was right. You are excellent at planning for the future."

"A lifetime of practice." He stood and held out his hand. "Ivy?"

"What, Hugh?"

"I'm shaky happy right now."

"I am too."

****

"Bellies full, gallons of coffee, a restroom break for each of us. Are you up for a short detour before we get the optics?"

"Of course, my love."

He led her to a gravel path winding up to the hill behind the parking lot, stopping when they reached the top. "This where the geolocator was found. On the gravel."

Ivy looked around. "How incredibly fortunate that it fell here, instead of in the deep woods. Or the ocean. And how amazing that anyone even saw it, a tiny gray thing on a lot of gray gravel."

"It is."

"This was a wonderful idea, Hugh, coming here. I like knowing that we're in the exact same spot that the Grace's Warbler was. Our warbler."

"You're convinced the geolocator came from that bird, aren't you?"

"Absolutely. Until I'm forced to admit it didn't." She turned toward him. "The first time I saw you as an interesting, thinking, feeling person was that day we watched the warbler in the back parking lot at the reservoir. I said I was touched that it was so alone and you agreed."

"I remember."

"And the first time I ever touched you was because of the warbler. And the first time you kissed me. On the ledge."

"We didn't kiss that day."

"You kissed the palm of my hand."

"Oh. That's right."

"And now we've followed that confused, lost little bird all the way to Newfoundland and we've decided to get married. It's like our totem bird."

"If you would like me to ask you in the traditional

way, Ivy, this would be the place to do it."

"Pardon?"

"On bended knee?"

"Oh. No. Definitely no."

"Whew."

"Whew, Hugh?" Her eyes widened. She giggled. "Why whew, Hugh?" Her giggles abruptly became helpless, on the knife-edge between laughing and sobbing. Hugh pulled her into his arms, his cheek against her hair, his hands smoothing her back and shoulders.

After many minutes, Ivy shuddered, took a deep breath, and leaned back. Her eyes glistened with humor and unshed tears. "I think I'm done with hysterics, at least for the moment."

"It's been an emotional morning."

"It has. And not enough sleep. And the…" She had to inhale sharply to ward off a second attack of giggles. "And the why-whew-Hugh bit was funny."

"It was."

She touched his cheek, her eyes suddenly somber. "And being angry is exhausting."

"I'm sorry, Ivy."

"Okay." She took another deep breath. "I'm going to try again, this time with impressive self-control. Why whew, Hugh?" Her voice quavered only a little.

"Stones."

"Pardon?"

"Kneeling here would hurt."

"Oh." She looked down at the sharp gray stones. "Ow."

"But I'm willing to, Ivy."

"No. This is our love story and it hasn't been traditional from the start."

"No."

"So no down on one knee. And you know? I don't think our wedding ceremony should be traditional either."

"I agree. Here's a thought." He tightened the muscles around his mouth and managed to look almost serious. "We could all hike up to that ledge. We'd say our vows and then we'd all hang glide back down, thus emulating the warbler."

"I don't think so, Hugh."

"Or we could ask everyone in the BBC to set out mist nets at every place that's important to us and catch scores of migrants and release them in a giant cloud just as we say our vows."

"I don't think so, Hugh."

"Have the ceremony where we went for that drawdown? Or in the field at the wildlife refuge?"

"I think it should be at our house. Our home."

"Yes. Excellent idea. We can ask the guests to cluster themselves way down at the corner of the block and watch the ceremony through their scopes and binocs."

"I don't think so, Hugh."

"We'll probably want to discuss this some more."

"I think so."

"But right now, Ivy…"

"Right now what, my love?"

He turned toward the gravel path, pulling her arm through his.

"Right now, sweetheart, let's go birding."

A word about the author...

Maeve Kim is a teacher, nature guide, gardener, musician, writer and well-known speaker. An earlier novel, There's Nothing 86 Tonight, was a popular book club choice, and her many articles about birds and birding have appeared in magazines and newspapers. She lives with her sweetheart in northern Vermont, where they maintain a blog called vtbirdsandwords.